Mercury Mountain

Reese ~
your mother
knows this
subject well!
- Enjoy the adventure!
India Evans

Mercury Mountain
An Eco-Adventure Series

By
INDIA EVANS

AuthorHouse™
1663 Liberty Drive, Suite 200
Bloomington, IN 47403
www.authorhouse.com
Phone: 1-800-839-8640

AuthorHouse™ UK Ltd.
500 Avebury Boulevard
Central Milton Keynes, MK9 2BE
www.authorhouse.co.uk
Phone: 08001974150

This book is a work of fiction. People, places, events, and situations are the product of the author's imagination. Any resemblance to actual persons, living or dead, or historical events, is purely coincidental.

First published by AuthorHouse 7/21/2006

ISBN: 1-4259-5443-X (sc)

Printed in the United States of America
Bloomington, Indiana

This book is printed on acid-free paper.

Cover and interior design by the Legwork Team.

*This book is dedicated to my husband, Alan,
who encouraged me to write and to my parents
who instilled in me a love of nature.*

Contents

Do no dishonor to the earth
lest you dishonor the spirit of man.

— Henry Beston, author of *The Outermost House,*
and renowned 20th-century American nature writer.

Saturday Morning

My eyes flew open. A dull clanging noise became louder and louder. Then, I heard, "Louie, take it easy with that can!"

I flung the pillow off my head and ran to the window. I peered down and saw the lawn strewn with garbage cans. Old banana peels, chicken bones, and paper wrappers trailed to the sidewalk, left to rot in the autumn warmth. I pushed open the window and shouted in a bullish voice, "Hey, your garbage stinks!" The garbage man gazed up and gave a quick cheerful wave. The truck he was riding on lurched to the next stop, spewing a cloud of exhaust behind.

The clock flashed 7:00 a.m. I stormed out of my bedroom and stumbled down the stairs, mumbling under my breath about the waste in this world. I entered the kitchen to see my wiry, ten-year old brother shoveling his breakfast — or as my mom calls it, "fast break" — into his mouth. His energy does not allow him to do anything slowly, and mealtime was no exception.

"Oh, you are disgusting," I said, pouring one of my mother's weird health concoctions into a bowl. This time it looked like oatmeal but tasted like blueberries.

"Children, can't we ever start one morning off quiet and calmly?" my mother asked.

"But Mom," I said, "look at him, he's an animal." We both turned to look at Cody, who struck an angelic pose. With his dirty blond locks still rumpled from sleep, even his hair resembled a halo. A messy halo, as if he put his hand in an electrical outlet.

My mother clapped her hands and said, "Okay, what's on your schedules for today? I am going to the clinic. Mrs. Johnson is bringing her entire Girl Scout troop in for a dental lesson and check-up. That should keep me tied up for most of the day. Cody?"

"I'm hanging with Sammy, and we're going skateboarding in the new park."

Mom turned to me, pulling back her hair that exactly matched my own strawberry blonde ponytail. "Julie?"

"Let's see." I rolled my eyes to the ceiling, looking for the plan of the day.

Cody jumped forward and jabbed me. "Hey, brainy sister, why don't you figure out why the garbage stinks?"

My mother ran her hand through the halo to smooth down the unruly strands of hair. She frowned with concern. "I do agree that the smell is horrible today."

"That's what happens when they don't cover the landfill correctly. I'm going to have to pay a visit. Thanks, Cody, for reminding me."

My dad walked quietly into the room. His glasses were a bit crooked on his face, and he looked puzzled. "Cody, did you get the mail from yesterday?"

Cody's fork hit the plate hard. He pushed himself away from the table. "Nah, haven't been able to. I've been busy."

My mother defended him, as usual. "Cody had some schoolwork he needed to finish. Julie, could you do us the favor?"

I nodded, took a last sip of fruit juice and grabbed my jacket.

Once I got outside, the chill of the New England air and the beauty of autumn hit me full force. The sun was just climbing into the cloudless sky. The trees looked as if someone had taken a vacuum to their edges but left the center intact. Their leaves glimmered in the soft breeze, mixing the various shades of gold, crimson, and jade. I grimaced when I smelled the odor of garbage hanging in the air.

I walked to the end of the driveway to our rusted mailbox. The door was ajar, and some of mail had tumbled out onto the lawn. I hastily bent over and retrieved the stray envelopes.

I got back inside, breezed by my brother, and tossed the pile on the table. My father darted out of the study and pounced on the stack of mail. "Julie, you have a letter," he said with a hint of surprise.

My hands trembled as I slid my finger under the flap of the expensive-looking envelope.

I tore it open, looking at my brother with smugness and importance. Inside was a formal letter with the company's embossed seal of a car with wings at the top.

I skimmed the letter, then shrieked as I jumped from my chair, knocking it over. I started dancing around, waving the letter high over my head.

"You won't believe this! I won! I won the car!"

The Letter

My father cleared his throat to make room for his serious voice, "Please don't leave us in suspense."

I started to read aloud.

Dear Julie Leeds:

It is with great pleasure that we award you first place in the Future Car Essay Contest. As the winner, you will receive a one-of-a-kind, eco-advanced automobile to aid in your studies centered on environmental challenges. Even though you are thirteen and under the legal driving age, you have been granted permission from the state to drive this vehicle for one year, granted that you comply with the guidelines of ownership (see enclosed document).

The contest drew over 500,000 entries nationwide, and we chose you because of your intelligent and meaningful essay. It clearly demonstrated how you would use the car to help clean up the environment and spread awareness of environmental issues in the community.

A representative will deliver the car to your home on October 2, and the master engineer will review all of the car features with you.

Congratulations on your achievement! We look forward to your accomplishments over the next year.
Sincerely,
FastTrack Motor Company, Grange Falls, USA

I shook my head in happy disbelief. "That's tomorrow!"

"Talk about short notice," my dad commented. "We need to figure out where to put this car." His salt and pepper hair was combed perfectly and didn't move as he turned to look at my mother.

I sashayed over to him. "We can make room in the garage, can't we? I'd be happy to help clean it out."

"We'll see," he said, as the lines on his forehead became more prominent. The news of my prize was quickly losing its excitement. Parents can ruin any surprise; just give them a few minutes.

My mother walked over and gave me a hug. "I'm proud of you! You deserve this award and the recognition. In celebration we are going out to dinner tonight. You name the place."

Did I mention they could be cool as well? At least one member of my family supports me.

Cody stood up and shouted, "Wait a minute! She can't drive a car, she's only thirteen!"

My father paused and then said to me, "You know, that could be a problem, but I have faith in you. Also, I just found out that your cousin, Cynthia is getting her learner's permit and she's only fifteen. Her state is trying to adopt a younger driving age to reward students."

I ran and hugged my father. I glanced over his shoulder and stuck my tongue out at Cody, as he slithered out of the room.

"If you'll excuse me, I want to tell Pete about this," I announced. As my best friend and partner in crime, I couldn't wait to tell him the news! Alone in my room, I quickly dialed the number to his phone. It kept ringing and finally on the fourth ring, he picked up. "Hello" he said in a sheepish voice.

"You'll never guess what happened this morning!"

"I can't imagine, given it's only seven-thirty."

Ignoring his snide remark, I replied, "Remember the contest I entered through the wildlife magazine?"

"You enter way too many contests. I can't keep track," he said impatiently.

"The future car one. You're talking to the new owner."

"Get out! How did you manage that?" his voice vibrated through the phone.

"Why do you think I joined the Environmental Visions and Energy Network with you?"

"Gee, I thought you joined E.V.E.N. because I was in it."

"You wish," I chuckled.

"When will I see you with the car?" he asked.

"I get it tomorrow. Oh, and I grant you exclusive story rights for the school paper."

"I can't wait! Catch you later," Pete said.

My head was spinning. Suddenly, I needed a minute to digest the news. I flopped onto my bed and stared at the star map on my ceiling. Right now, I couldn't think of anything I wanted to do more than dream about my new car!

3

From a Land Down Under

"Julie, Julie, Julie," my brother yelled as he ran over to me. "Where is it?" He stuck his head in front of mine to peer out the living room window.

I held my breath as I watched a gigantic truck park in front of the house. I wiped the perspiration from my upper lip; it felt like the middle of summer on this Sunday afternoon in New England. I had already changed my clothes three times.

When the doorbell rang, our labrador retriever dog, Magic started barking wildly, and Cody had to usher him into another room. I checked my outfit in the mirror and smoothed my hair before I opened the door.

There stood two very different-looking men. One was tall, attractive, and well dressed. He extended his delicate hand and said formally, "My name is Charles Lakehorn; I'm with the FastTrack Motor Company."

"Hi. I'm Julie." I smiled and turned to the other man, who shifted back and forth as if the energy in him couldn't be contained. He was older and stocky, with receding dark brown hair and large sea-green eyes. He cleared his throat and said warmly, in an Australian accent, "Greetings, mate. I'm PJ Riley. I'm the master engineer of your new car. Congratulations!"

I stood in the doorway staring at them. Cody ran up next to me and burst out, "Where's the car?"

I started to giggle as Charles smoothed his tailored pinstriped gray suit and glanced at my brother. "Excellent question, young fellow," he said and then looked at me. "Julie, would you like to see your car?"

"Yes, of course," I replied.

We followed closely as they led us across the lawn to the 18-wheeler. The driver had already opened the back door and had assembled the tire ramps to remove the car. PJ whistled for its release.

As quickly as the sun sets on a winter evening, my life changed in an instant and all of the sounds around me became muted. I stared in awe as the car slowly rolled down the ramp. This was the coolest car I had ever seen.

The first thing that caught my eye was the way the shiny metallic paint glistened in the afternoon sun. The shape of the car was unlike any I had ever seen. It was a two-door sports car mounted on a thin frame shaped like a surfboard; long and lean and low to the ground with the midsection bowed out slightly. The windows were tinted, which made it nearly impossible to see inside. The front headlights lived in a casing that was one with the hood of the car. It had a rear trunk and a back oval window that was framed by two rounded rear lights.

There was something unique about the car that

I couldn't quite place. It almost looked as if the car was breathing!

PJ waved his arm over the car, like a magician introducing a trick. "Here's your car! What do you think?"

Cody elbowed me in the arm, prompting me to reply.

"I, ah, it's amazing!"

"What kind of car is it?" Cody questioned, as my parents joined us.

"The codename is Jett," PJ replied. "It stands for Justified Environmental Talking Technology. Basically it means the car can talk."

I shrieked, "It can what?"

I looked at Cody and saw his eyes light up.

PJ continued casually, "We've outfitted the car with the 8X A.I. chip, so your driving experience will be a learning and interactive one."

My parents' mouths dropped wide open, and my heart skipped a beat. After my father paced around the car a few times, he asked, "Let me get this straight, sir. The car has the ability to converse?"

"That's correct." Charles grinned. "Don't worry, it won't bite."

"Why don't we all take a ride?" PJ suggested. "To make you feel more comfortable." He motioned for me to sit in the driver's seat. I eagerly jumped in and leaned back into the cushy seat.

My parents climbed into the back seat as PJ vaulted into the passenger's seat as if he was a kid. Cody stayed with Charles, waiting his turn for the next ride.

I glanced out of the tinted windows to see some of my neighbors standing in their yards looking at us. I smiled.

"Now for the fun part." PJ laughed loudly, his round belly expanding in and out.

"The driving?" I asked.

"Well, there's that, yes, but you need to be introduced first." he declared. He pointed to the computer screen mounted where a rear view mirror would typically go. "You'll need to touch this to activate all of Jett's senses. This way he can communicate with you."

I touched the screen, and the car instantly came to life.

PJ said, "Jett, mate, I want you to meet your new owner." He gestured that I should speak.

I whispered, "Hi Jett. I'm Julie."

A friendly, male voice inside the car responded, "Greetings, mate, I'm honored to serve you."

PJ turned to everyone and said, "We've been rehearsing that one all week."

Everyone laughed. PJ blushed.

"Hey, did I notice an Australian accent?" I asked.

"Yes indeed. He was programmed through voice recognition. It was inevitable that Jett would pick up my accent."

"I like it. It makes him seem human," I said.

PJ showed me how to work the automatic gearshift. As soon as I put the car in reverse, a lightweight, see-through safety harness automatically attached itself around me. The computer screen flickered.

PJ pointed to the screen. "You'll notice that the car provides a view of the road ahead. But if you hit this button, it shows the views on all four sides." He glanced back at my parents, "Another feature, which I'm sure you'll find comforting, is that Jett can broadcast what's happening in the car to any television or computer screen you request."

"Can we talk to one another as well?" my mother asked.

"Of course. That's the beauty of the system. Interactive access all the time," PJ replied.

I cringed at this remark. That's all I needed, my parents keeping an eye on me in the car.

"I don't want Julie to be distracted when she drives." My mom said and turned to my dad, "Don't you think she should just check in with us on a routine basis?"

My father sighed. "I agree, but we'll have to see how well that works."

Suddenly Jett said, "Trash alert."

I looked at PJ. "What does that mean?"

"Jett is programmed to notice any disturbance in the environment, whether it's trash on the side of the road or a sudden rain shower."

"Unbelievable," my father commented, shaking his head in amazement.

PJ nodded. "Feel free to ask Jett anything. His memory bank holds more information about the environment than Mother Nature."

"This promises to be interesting," I said.

"And don't forget fun!" my mother added. She looked as delighted as a child at an amusement park.

We drove along the main road through my quaint New England town to the only major highway around.

"Caution," said Jett as I tugged on the wheel a bit too far to the right, and we started to veer to the side of the road. The wheel started to move in my hands as Jett made us stay in line.

"What just happened?" I asked.

"Jett pays attention to everything you do. If he senses you are going off the road or going to hit another car, he'll take over and make sure you avoid any unpleasant situation," PJ said.

"Learning how to drive just got easier!" I laughed.

Once we were on the highway, I started to get antsy and wanted to see how fast Jett could go. My parents were engrossed in a conversation with PJ, so I took my chance by pushing down on the accelerator. I watched as the digital dial started climbing. If it weren't for the fact that cars in the other lanes looked like they were standing still, I would have sworn we were going the same speed. It was that smooth. My heart started beating rapidly.

"Julie," PJ said with an edge in his voice, "aren't we going a bit too fast?" I edged off the pedal and said, "I was just testing Jett."

"You might want to remember to conserve on gas," my mother said.

PJ grinned. "Only one problem with that Mrs. Leeds, it doesn't run on gasoline. It uses a hydrogen fuel-cell, which makes it a clean-burning engine."

"The only type of exhaust that comes out of the tailpipe is water," I added.

A half-hour later, we pulled into my driveway. "Those are the basics," PJ said. He paused, "There's one other feature that only this model car has."

My father's eyebrows arched. "You mean besides the fact that it can talk?"

PJ grinned. "Let's get out and I'll show you."

Cody and Charles joined us as I scrambled to help my parents out of the back seat. I couldn't wait to find out more.

"See this latch underneath the tire base?" PJ pointed to the rear tire. "The outer shell snaps into the chassis."

"If it snaps in, it must snap off," my father said.

"Yes, Mr. Leeds, you got that right. In essence, this car can also be a truck, a sports car, a sedan, you name it."

"Wow! A car that comes with disguises," I said.

PJ then explained where to get the car serviced in case we wanted to change the look.

My mother interrupted. "All this fancy talk is making me thirsty. Can I get anyone something to drink?"

We all nodded.

PJ nudged me, "Why don't Julie and I get the drinks?"

"That's nice of you to offer, but I shouldn't have a problem," she said with a smile.

"I insist," he said firmly. "Plus, this will give you

more time to inspect the car and ask me any questions when I return."

We started to walk towards the house. PJ touched my arm and said softly, "Julie, I have something very important I need to tell you about Jett."

4

The Secret

I showed PJ into the kitchen.

He scanned the room to make sure we were alone and then spoke in a low voice. "I wanted to make this car superior to any other car in the world. I wanted it to be stylish, safe, and smart."

"I think you've accomplished that!" I said puzzled. What could he want to tell me?

He frowned slightly. "However, I realized it could also be dangerous."

"What do you mean?" I took a pitcher of lemonade from the fridge.

"In order for Jett to provide information on the environment, I had to create a computer system that could connect with computers and satellites all over the world. Basically, he has the ability to control things."

"That's pretty wild!" I declared. "But what does that mean to me?"

"It means this machine has the power to change things." He paused and then added, "and if it gets into the wrong hands, it could be very bad."

My heart sank. This was major league. I'd felt so

exhilarated driving, and now this. Grown-ups are just too serious! Ugh!

Sensing my despair, PJ smiled kindly. "No worries, love. Nothing bad will happen."

"I hope not," I answered, rolling my eyes up to the sky in prayer.

He reached for my hand and placed a slim micro disc in it. "If you sense you are in danger, insert this into the onboard computer, and it will lock the system."

I nodded and forced myself to swallow. I had to remind myself why I had become interested in the environment to begin with.

As if he read my mind, he said, "Julie, if you don't mind my asking, why are you on this environmental crusade?"

I met his curious gaze. His face was tanned and wrinkled from the Australian sun. "My grandparents are the reason."

I arranged some glasses on a tray and explained as I poured the lemonade. "They lived on a hundred-acre farm. I loved it there. They taught me to farm and preserve nature's resources. Until one day."

His eyes grew large. "What happened?"

"A nearby factory contaminated their water supply. The animals got sick and started to die off. To make matters worse, litter and car exhaust from a new highway started to harm the crops. By the time the state finished their investigation, my grandparents were in the hospital, and a short time later they passed away."

His eyes dropped and he said, "I'm sorry, Julie."

"From that day on, I vowed to my parents that I would do whatever I could to clean up the environment. They supported me on one condition."

"Which was?"

"To make my schoolwork my number one priority."

"A wise request. I like your parents. They seem very open to new ideas."

I lowered my voice. "I'm lucky. I guess."

"Don't sound disappointed, mate." He grinned. "You are lucky. And smart enough to know it."

I couldn't help feeling guilty. I was the winner of this amazing super car, which I could drive legally and I was stuck on complaining about my parents. I needed to snap out of it!

"Hey, PJ, what's it like in Australia?"

He picked up the tray of glasses. "Magnificent. We have beaches, mountains, the desert, the famous 'outback', you name it."

"And the people?"

"We are extremely proud of our country and we tend to make fun of everything and everyone. It's part of our laid-back style."

I remembered reading something about how Australians were quite happy to tell their life story. "Do you have family in Australia?" I asked.

His body tensed, and then he replied, "Yes and no. My parents are no longer living, but my two brothers are still there."

"Do you have your own family?"

He shrugged. "No, I was always so busy working that I didn't have time to spend with anyone. Jett was my family for awhile and now he'll be part of yours."

He motioned with his chin for me to open the door. We headed out with the drinks.

I wanted to know more about PJ, but my father pointed to our neighbor and shouted, "Julie, Mr. Rollins wanted to know about your new car."

I introduced PJ to him and told him about the contest.

"You are one lucky girl," he said with his hands buried deep in his pockets. "So, do you think you can solve our local garbage problem? Do you know where the smell originates?"

All eyes were on me as I pulled a stray piece of hair behind my ear, a nervous habit of mine. "I wish I did, Mr. Rollins. I'm going to investigate the landfill as soon as I can; don't you worry."

"Please do. You've been very helpful in the past. First with the bee problem and then the water situation."

PJ and Charles raised their eyebrows.

"I will let you know," I said, hoping Mr. Rollins would stop embarrassing me.

After my parents and Cody went inside to finish chores, I had a final review of the car. Charles had to leave because of a sales meeting, and I was alone with PJ once again.

"PJ, thanks for everything, you've been great!" I said.

"Ah, you're a love."

"Any last words of advice?" I asked.

"Beware of tall poppies," he replied.

"What are those?"

"People who think they are more important than anyone else or anything. You call them 'snobs' in America. My father never trusted anyone who thought they were better than others. Selfishness happens to be the direct cause of our environmental problems. People need to realize that their actions affect us all."

"I'll keep it in mind. Good-bye, PJ." I gave him a hug.

He hoisted himself into the truck. The engine roared to life, and I waved as it went down the road.

I gazed at Jett in the driveway. I wanted to pinch myself. The car was all mine!

I skipped toward the garage to start cleaning when a stray piece of trash in the grass caught my eye. I reached down to pick it up. It was a weathered piece of newspaper. I unraveled it and read out loud the article's headline: "Learn to Grow Poppies the Easy Way."

It was as if PJ had left it on purpose.

"Nice wheels!" A voice called out behind me.

I felt a hand on my shoulder and jumped. I turned quickly to see Pete standing there with his notebook.

"Yikes, you scared me."

"Didn't mean to." Pete walked over to Jett and ran his hand across the front of the hood. "I never saw this material before. It has a much different feel than steel. Pretty amazing. Are you ready to give me a tour of the car?"

I nodded, tucking the piece of newspaper into my back pocket, and said, "There are many unusual things about this car. Jett, say hello to Pete."

5

First Ride

Jett Log: 7.00 hrs.

Long hours had passed. Finally, she opened the garage door with the touch of a button. The instant she saw me, her smile radiated from her pretty little face that peeked out from under her baseball hat. Her blue eyes lit up the room.

"Hi, Jett," she said with excitement in her voice. "Are you ready to take a drive?" I sure was. I had been parked in this cold, concrete box all night. And I was bloody bored.

Just as I was about to answer, we both heard the side door from the house open. Cody, dressed in a ripped polo shirt and baggy jeans, whined, "Julieeee, you said you would give me a ride!"

His slight body raced to the driver's side and he proceeded to bump Julie, who was holding the door open, out of the way.

"Cody!" Julie said nervously. "I can't drive you today. I'm picking up my friend, Pete. And by the way, what are you doing?"

"Relax, sis, I'm just checking it out," he replied as his sweaty fingers started pressing the buttons on my steering wheel. Looking at the spacious interior, he asked, "Hey, why doesn't this car have an engine in the front?"

"Because it is a fuel-cell car. Didn't you listen to a word PJ said yesterday?"

She had a right to be annoyed. But I'm sure the little terror doesn't really care about the new ways to power automobiles. Cody was entranced with my interior. "Wow, there are tons of buttons and cool gadgets. What's this for?"

"I can show you all this later. I'm kind of in a rush," Julie pleaded.

"How fast does it go?" Cody gazed at the digital speedometer.

"This car is much lighter and more aerodynamic than other cars. It can accelerate from zero to sixty miles per hour in less than ten seconds and goes as fast as 150 miles per hour," she answered with a glint of pride.

"Very cool." Cody nodded in approval.

I listened to the questions that Cody was asking Julie, hoping this meddling monster would leave soon. I wanted to stretch my wheels. I soon realized that he wasn't bright enough to take a hint. I'd have to use my own voice to scare him off.

"Ready to ride?" I blared.

Cody jumped and hit his head on my inside roof.

"Cody, I can't believe that scared you. You know he can talk." Julie observed.

"Ah, I forgot," he said, rubbing his head, and quickly hoisted himself out of the front seat.

Julie rumpled his hair. "Sorry. I'll take you for a ride tomorrow."

"Maybe," he mumbled with his back to Julie as he walked toward the door leading to the house.

Julie grinned as she plopped into the driver's seat and said, "Jett, I've got to watch you. I keep forgetting that you see and hear everything."

"I was only trying to help," I replied.

"Yes, but I can handle my brother."

"Okay, I'll be good."

"Can we get moving? We need to visit the landfill this morning. This smell worsens by the minute," she said.

After she touched the screen, my engine came to life with a low humming sound. The lights on the steering wheel lit up in a light green hue. My wheels reversed out of the garage, and we were on our way.

As we drove through the sleepy neighborhood, we passed large, stately oak trees and homes that were set wide apart and far from the road I asked, "Julie, don't you have school today?"

Her eyes twinkled. "Yes, but it is extremely important that I find out what is going on at the landfill. Something isn't right. In a typical landfill, they cover all of the garbage with dirt to prevent odors and to help keep away animals and bugs."

I knew this fact, but I was more concerned that she might get in trouble. "Do your parents know you are paying a visit to the landfill?"

Julie started pulling on a stray piece of hair behind

her left ear. "No, but I'm going straight to school afterwards."

This wasn't a good sign. She was already lying to her parents.

A Landfill Lead

We drove through the heart of my town, with its traditional white church, general store, town hall, and post office. Soon we reached the rolling green fields of farm country. It was laid out like nature's picnic basket. The lushness was comforting and serene in the early months of autumn. Signs along the road said, 'Caution, Cattle Crossing,' or 'Pick Your Own Strawberries.' Then, I saw the one sign that didn't belong, a tiny, yellow sign that read: Regents Landfill 1 Mile Ahead.

When I became a member of E.V.E.N. (Environmental Visions Energy Network), my first assignment was to investigate the amount and type of garbage that was being produced in my town.

Testing Jett's knowledge, I asked, "Hey, Jett, did you know that each person in the United States throws out about ten pounds of garbage every day?"

He responded, "Julie, are you asking me about garbage? You humans are walking waste generators. For instance, each hour, people in this country use three and a half million plastic bottles. Garbage in the U.S. fills 500,000 garbage trucks a day. That's just staggering."

"How about a big city?"

"There's the Big Apple for one... more like rotten apple in my book. It throws out enough trash to fill the Empire State Building two times over every week."

"Jett, don't be hard on New York City. There are just a lot of people living there. At least they use public transportation."

"Now I suppose you'll want me to answer the question, Why a landfill?"

"Yes, that was my next question."

"A landfill provides a cleaner way of decomposing trash and is safer for the environment than a typical garbage dump. But don't be fooled by the word 'cleaner'. There are still problems involved in keeping the trash out of the land and water supply."

"Do you know the reason they opened the landfill here in town?"

"That I do not, Miss Julie, please tell me."

"A couple of years ago, I started a campaign to remind people about the recycling program. Unfortunately, many people didn't take it seriously, and they had to open the Regents Landfill to take care of the mounting trash."

A short distance away, the road dead-ended at the landfill. The entrance housed a security office. The small building was reinforced with bars on the windows and triple locks at the door; all that was missing was the token weathered watchdog. An extremely high chain-link fence surrounded the landfill. Signs on the fence warned, "No Trespassing" and "No Illegal Dumping."

I honked the horn and Gil, the security guard, came slowly out of the office.

Gil reminded me of a chameleon. He was tall and thin and parted his hair to the right, allowing his dark, greasy bangs to hide his protruding eyes. He had been a fixture in the community for over ten years, but no one really knew him.

"Hi, Gil. I've come to find out about the horrible smell that's hanging over the town," I called out to him.

Gil hovered over the car window, smelling of stale cigarettes. "Hey, Julie. I heard about your fancy new car. How are you?" He smiled, exposing his yellow, stained teeth.

"Not good, Gil. What's the source of the smell?"

"It started a few days ago. We had about four loads of waste from the folks who are putting in the new housing development. Maybe that triggered something."

"Do you mind if I take a sample?"

"I'd have to check with the boss, but he's on vacation." Gil paused, then said, "It should be all right." He beckoned with his gloved hand toward the reinforced gate, then disappeared into the office to unlock it.

As we drove through the gate, the air in the landfill felt thicker and the smell grew worse. It caught in my throat as I coughed to clear it. I flicked on the filtered air switch.

"Jett, did you get a picture of Gil on one of your digital cameras?" I asked after I caught my breath.

"Yes, I've got it stored in my memory," Jett responded.

Jett seemed to hum as we drove down the stony road toward the mounds of trash.

"Jett, what do you think of Gil?"

"Interesting fella. He seems shifty," Jett responded.

"Ah, yes," I said. "What about the landfill?"

Jett did a quick analysis and responded, "The landfill measures twenty acres in size. It has a truck weighing station to record the amounts of waste coming in; a large mound of soil in the east corner to cover material being dumped; a treatment area for leachate, which is a composition of garbage and rainwater; and an area where people can drop off hazardous waste materials. For the most part, it's your standard operation."

I slowed Jett to a stop and put on rubber-insulate gloves with Velcro to protect my skin from the decaying material.

I got out of the car to begin the testing process right from Jett's trunk. The test is called GEOS, which stands for "general environmental one step." It's used to test for harmful materials found in the soil. In order to take the GEOS test, a computer chip, which we call a "bulb," is placed deep in the soil to read what ingredients are present. "Ok, Jett, send it down."

A compartment in the trunk opened instantly and produced a small container shaped like an arrowhead. It plunged about fifty feet into the soil. I glanced at my watch to keep an eye on the time. After three minutes, the electronic arm came back up and did a self-clean before I loaded it back into a compartment in the car. The bulb had gotten the soil sample data.

After I jumped into the driver's seat, I peeled off my gloves. I inserted the bulb into a specially designed slot on the dashboard and reviewed the testing time, air temperature, and procedure data that appeared on the computer screen. "Great job, Jett!"

"Piece of cake. The test will tell us what lies in the soil and how long it's been there," Jett said.

As we slowly made our way back to the entrance, something caught my eye over a small hill. Some vultures and crows were diving into a trash heap. They seemed to be carrying small pieces of plastic.

"Jett, I think we found the origin of the smell," I said, "Let's get closer!"

A large hole was exposed, not only causing the intense smell but also attracting all types of wildlife and insects. There were dozens of computer and electronic parts intertwined with decaying garbage.

When we reached the gates, Gil waved me to slow down. His eyes narrowed, and he pointed to the police car that was parked outside of the office. "You have company," he said.

I glared at Gil. "What's he doing here?"

"I forgot to mention the security cameras are hooked up to the police station. They must have spotted you," he answered, lowering his head and rounding his shoulders like a dog being scolded by his owner.

Suddenly, a burly police officer was standing next to my door. "Good morning, Miss," he said. "Can I ask what you are doing on private property?"

"I was just testing soil for a school project."

He looked down at his watch, adjusted his sunglasses, and surveyed the car, "So you're the kid that won the car. You may be allowed to drive at thirteen, but you still have to go to school like everyone else."

"Um, I'm on my way," I said and then added, "Sir."

"I'm going to make this a warning, but the next time I'll have to give you a fine for trespassing. Understood?"

"Yes, officer, I understand completely." I could feel the sweat on the back of my neck. That was close!

His boots were heavy on the gravel drive as he walked back to his patrol car. My heart was pounding and I had to breathe in deeply to calm down. He waved for me to go ahead of him. I hesitated, then instructed Jett to drive toward the school.

"Jett, do you think Gil called the police?"

"I can check for you."

"Right, I forgot you could do that. Please do."

In an instant his computer hooked up with the local phone company and began scanning by location and phone number.

"Bingo. Our friend Gil did indeed call the police."

"That's very interesting. Why does he care if I go in the 'fill? He let me in, didn't he?

"Maybe he wanted to discourage you from coming back."

7

Jaded Jonathan

Atlas Jr. High was a suburban middle school with over four hundred students from three districts. The school was located on the outskirts of town and was laid out like a college campus. A central courtyard was the showpiece for sculptures that the students had created. It also contained a stone fountain shaped in the form of the school's mascot, a phoenix.

I drove into the parking lot and maneuvered Jett as far away from the building as possible. I did not want Jonathan Weld to see the car. Jonathan was your typical bully, always picking on people half his size and making their lives miserable with pranks and name-calling.

I had nicknamed him 'Jaded Jonathan' because he was bored with most everything and everyone. His parents were inventors and he always had the most advanced gadgets.

As I opened the beige side door to the school with the soccer ball prints on it, I spotted Jonathan down the hall. He was tall with light brown hair that had been shaved like a military cut. His mouth seemed too big for his face and his voice was loud and commanded attention. He was leaning over a group of boys, showing them some type of device. As the door banged behind me, his head immediately went up and he screeched, "Juuuulie," as it echoed down the hall. "Come here, I have something for you."

I scowled at his foreboding frame blocking the middle of the hallway. "Not today, Jonathan, I have to study for a test." I looked for another hallway to escape down, but there were none on this side of the building.

"Take your test and shove it," he shouted abrasively. "I have something you'd really like for that nifty car of yours." I swallowed hard.

All eyes were upon me as I walked the runway of dread. I heard whispers among kids who were standing near him.

As I got close, he leered at me and said, "I wanted you to hang this inside your car. To make sure you'll think of me." He dangled a pair of fuzzy, white dice in his large hands, but these were no ordinary dice. Inserted into one side of the dice was a small video screen. It displayed a crude image of Jonathan 'mooning' the camera. The bully shoved the dice into my face.

I grabbed them and shrieked, throwing them to the ground, hoping he would think I'd turned red from anger, not embarrassment. I said forcefully, "Jonathan, you are completely disgusting."

He laughed loudly. A few boys laughed as well, but they sounded ill at ease.

I felt like a caged animal. I ran past him down the hall as fast as I could.

I rounded the corner and saw Pete from a distance

trying to organize the mess of books he had piled up in his locker. He was dressed in a plaid shirt and a pair of beige pants.

"Pete," I cried, breathing heavily, "Thank God you are here."

"Hey, slow down. What's going on? You don't look that well," he replied, his green eyes were quizzical.

"It was Jonathan again. He totally embarrassed me in front of all his friends."

"Wow. What a jerk. You've done nothing to him."

"Maybe I should do something to him."

"Whoa, rebel. That doesn't sound like you." Pete shook his head.

"There's got to be something I could do. You know, to send a message," I said.

I looked up as a loud group of girls came walking down the corridor toward us. They breezed by without a glance or acknowledgement. But one girl stopped. It was Gisele Nickels, one of the most popular girls in the ninth grade.

Her petite frame, long blonde hair, and delicate features made her a favorite with the boys.

The air filled with her light floral scent as she approached. "Hey, Julie, I heard about what just happened. Jonathan is a total creep."

"Gisele, why are you talking to her?" one of her friends hissed from a few feet away.

Ignoring her remark, she replied, "Go ahead, Cindy, I'll meet you in class."

I stood there, speechless.

"You know, there is one thing you can do to get back at him," she said, as her amber eyes narrowed.

Out of the corner of my eye, I noticed a slight grin from Pete. I asked shyly, "Oh, what might that be?"

"Since he's jealous of your car, maybe you should start giving people rides in it and exclude him," she offered.

The thought lingered for an instant like a soap bubble floating in the air, and then we were interrupted by a school bell ringing, signaling the start of the first class.

"Good idea, Gisele. I'll think about it," I answered. Darn, why did I hesitate? I sounded like an idiot. Facing Pete, I said, "I've gotta run. I'll catch you later?"

"Sure thing," he said.

"See ya, Julie." Gisele waved slightly as she sauntered into her class.

The morning went by slowly as my mind drifted to thoughts of Jett and the landfill episode that morning. Who was dumping those electronics? I needed to get to the bottom of this. And why, of all people, did Gisele take the time of day to talk to me? That was odd.

Finally, lunchtime rolled around and I had a chance to catch up with Pete again. "Can you meet me at the E.V.E.N. lab after school to double-check the soil sample?" I asked.

"Sure, I can make time for it before my story for the paper is due."

I swung my backpack over my shoulder and tucked loose strands of hair behind my ear. I took a minute to study Pete as he arranged items in his locker; his dirty blonde hair always looked ruffled and hid his boyish round face.

He sensed my stare and said quickly, "By the way, I was meaning to ask you, what was with Gisele? She never talks to anyone outside of her group."

"Maybe she just feels sorry for me," I said.

Pete chuckled. "Yeah. Or maybe she just wants a ride in your car."

Lab Scare

Jett Log: 13.00 hrs.

My internal clock knew it was the end of the school day, and I heard the soft tap and slide of her shoes hitting the pavement a few minutes later. Yippee!

I didn't like it when Julie was at school. Sitting in the parking lot was boring. I saw and heard the whole world around me bustling. I need to be out there observing and monitoring the environment. Darn kid. Couldn't she see that I needed to be active? Wasn't that in the training? I might start losing some of my circuitry just sitting around.

She opened the door and touched the computer screen. "Jett, we need to go to the Environmental Visions and Energy Network lab. I'll program in the location for you."

"Go right ahead," I replied, as my computer set up the trip mode.

She slumped into the driver's seat.

"Anything bothering you?" I asked.

"I had a horrible day at school, thanks to Jonathan Weld," she said. "It all started because he found out about you."

"I'm the hornet in his pants?"

"What?" she asked stunned.

"You know, the log dragging him down, the kick in his butt, the..."

"I got it, I got it," she interrupted with a note of delight in her voice. "Yes, he's unhappy that his parents didn't invent something like you for him. Talk about incredibly spoiled."

"A cheeky dandy, we Australians would call him."

"Oooh, that sounds too nice."

"Not coming from an Australian. If something sounds good you can assume it means the opposite."

"Tell me more about these dandy's. What do you say to them to make them stop?"

"We like to get them in situations where they aren't the center of attention."

"Such as...?"

"That depends on what that person considers attention. Each dandy is different, but deep down they are all the same — chasing away loneliness."

She chatted more about Jonathan, her classes, and her friend, Pete and then we were there. Darn! As I turned into the entrance and drove toward the front of the building, I saw Pete leaning against a stand-up cart supported by two large wheels, an electric scooter that looked like a modern-day chariot without the horse. Julie pressed my horn button, and he looked up from fixing his scooter.

"Hey, Pete," she called out the window.

More like puny Pete. Too bad this kid wasn't very

tall. No wonder Julie had the bullies after her. This one sure wasn't going to scare them off. I'll give him one thing; he was cute in an odd sort of way. Julie had told me that she met Pete through the E.V.E.N. agency and that they are now best friends. I remember all of the questions he was asking Julie on the first day I was dropped off. What a nosy guy, but, then again, he is a journalist. All I can say is, he'd better be nice to her.

"How's it going with motor mouth?" Pete asked.

What a wise guy.

Julie smiled and replied, "I've been learning some interesting things."

"Such as?" Pete asked.

"That they call kids like Jonathan 'cheeky dandies' in Australia," she said.

"Oh, how brilliant!" Pete replied. They both laughed, and I couldn't help but feel good at the mileage I got out of that one.

Julie glanced at her watch. "We'd better get going. I know you have a paper to write," Julie said, grabbing her bag that contained the sample. "We'll be out in awhile, Jett."

I guessed I'd have to get used to this waiting around nonsense.

The E.V.E.N. lab was an old warehouse building converted into office space. There were three floors, with the lab on the first, offices and a boardroom on the second, and a library on the top floor. The top floor had large skylights with a garden in the middle of the library. Pete and I usually did our homework up there because it was quiet.

As we entered the front lobby, Sabrina a dark-haired, college student who was a lab assistant, greeted us. After a quick hello, I dashed over to my lab station and used my fingerprint to start my computer. Pete lingered in the reception area talking with Sabrina about the story he was writing on the government.

I downloaded the data that Jett had captured from this morning's experiment. Suddenly, the lights flickered and dimmed, and then everything went black! I jumped in my chair and fell backwards on the floor with a thud. Stunned, I quickly got up and looked around. The other computers had gone out as well. "Oh, no!" I cried.

Pete and Sabrina came rushing over. He took a look at my chair lying on the floor and asked, "Are you okay?"

"I think so," I said, smoothing my wrinkled shirt. "I hope I didn't damage the system."

"No problem. We have emergency back-up on everything," Sabrina responded.

Pete pointed to a glass-enclosed room at the back of the lab. "I'm going to check out the damage."

Sabrina nodded. "You do that, and I'll go upstairs to see if anyone else was affected."

Moments later he sprinted back to my computer station. "Looks like our culprit was an outsider. The security block was completely shut down, which happens to be one of the hardest things to crack. I think the system is safe now, but we might have lost some data. You should run a test of what you just entered."

As I checked what I had just downloaded, the computer responded with a quiet churning sound. Within seconds the information came back on the screen — all was secure. I turned to see Pete looking out the window intently.

"Thanks for helping out. What would I do without you?"

"Maybe Jett could have helped you out," he said, a little sarcastically.

"I don't think so. He couldn't have worked the system the way you..." I stopped myself, remembering what PJ had told me. Jett was sophisticated enough to protect the lab computers and erase any wrongdoings. Amazing!

"After all this, didn't you have something to tell me?" Pete asked.

"Oh right. The soil readings revealed high amounts of mercury, cadmium, and lead."

"Isn't mercury found in computers?"

"Yes, and lead is used in TV and computer monitors, and cadmium is found in batteries," I said.

"Aaah, talk about serious stuff, Jules," Pete said. "I know for sure the government enacted a law over a year ago that makes it illegal to dump electronics into landfills. I just finished an article on environmental laws, and this one was mentioned."

"Yes, the law is based on the amount of computers being thrown away. Over 500 million computers were disposed of in the past ten years alone," I explained.

"I thought this type of material was sent overseas to companies to recycle the parts."

"Some is, but as you can see, some remains. And there was a mountain of it at Regents," I answered.

"The thing we need to find out now is whether these poisonous materials are seeping into the soil and the groundwater."

Pete's eyes widened. "Before you get all Detective on me, can you help me by reviewing my article on local companies for the school paper?"

"Oh right. I forgot. Better yet, why don't you have Jett read it?" I offered. Pete flashed me a stern look. I grabbed his notebook. "On second thought, I'll give it a read right now."

I took some time to read the article. On the last page there was a review about a computer warehouse store.

"Whoa! I completely forgot about this place. It's the perfect place to start."

"The CHIPDOME?" he asked.

"Yes, they have a recycling program. I'm curious to see how it works."

"In other words, you want to snoop," he said.

"Yes, right down your alley!" I answered. I couldn't wait to start!

Jett Log: 17.00 hrs.

She looked like the cat that had swallowed the canary as she emerged from the lab. I wasn't quite sure if she would divulge the computer problem. I didn't even know if her friend would have the sense to figure it out.

Julie quickly dialed her home phone number.

"Dad! I'm on my way home," Julie said.

"How are you and Jett doing?" he asked.

"We're doing just fine."

They talked about the day's news and school projects and then Julie switched the monitor on. "Jett, home please," she instructed me.

"On our way," I replied.

She then asked, "Jett did you help out in the lab when the computers went down?"

I couldn't lie about this one. Bloody kid. "Why yes, I did. Everything all right?" Maybe I could play dumb.

"Fine, I just didn't realize how advanced you were until this happened."

"PJ did give me some helpful features," I answered.

"Okay movie star, now do you have any idea who was trying to shut down the computers?"

"My guess is it was someone who has government security clearance or someone familiar with the E.V.E.N. lab computer system," I said.

"How is it that you prevented this?" Julie tilted her head, her eyes narrowed.

"My computer is designed to foresee and predict problems, so as soon as I logged into the lab's system, I detected that someone had already scheduled the system to go down. There was nothing I could do to stop it, so I made sure I protected all that I could."

"So the wheels were in motion?"

"Precisely."

She nodded and I noticed her shoulders relax.

"Can you let me know if I'll get into Harvard?"

"I may be about to predict a future outcome, but I'm no miracle worker."

She laughed and said, "Thanks for the vote of confidence."

A Warning

As I walked into the house, I noticed the flicker of images from the large flat screen television illuminating the den. Cody was busy attacking his video game controller with his right hand and digging his left hand into a bowl of chips.

In the kitchen, I caught a glimpse of my mother shuffling back and forth, adjusting her headset. Her words were muffled, but I made out something about taking care of gums. This would be very strange in most households, but you see, my mother owns her own dental practice. I headed for my father's study, where the sounds of his deep breathing confirmed he was sleeping on the couch.

I enjoyed spending time in his cozy study. It had comfortable furniture, lush carpeting, a fireplace, and dark maple bookshelves that were built into the wall from floor to ceiling. A sliding door led out onto a tiny patio my mother had claimed as her "rose terrace." Unfortunately, it didn't have a single rose growing on it. She never found the time to plant them.

As I tiptoed near him, his eyes opened slightly and then focused. "Oh, there you are sweetie," he said.

"How's the car?"

"Pretty cool. I'm learning so much," I replied.

Cody interrupted. "Well, if it isn't my sister, the wimp!" He strutted into the room with his hands shoved into his pockets.

I cringed. "What are you talking about?"

"My friend Jim told me all about how you ran down the hall because Jonathan made fun of you and the car."

"It's no secret that Jonathan envies me," I said defensively.

"Excuse me," my father intervened. "Julie, I think there is something we have to discuss. Cody, ten more minutes on that game and then you have to do your homework."

I turned to give Cody a dirty look. He stuck his tongue out on his way back to the TV.

My father leaned toward me. "I got a call today from someone by the name of Gil. Does that name ring a bell?"

I felt my face flush. "Ah, yes. He manages the landfill," I stammered.

"He mentioned that you took some kind of sample this morning."

I cleared my throat and said, "Yes, I needed to investigate where the smell was coming from. As it turns out, there are mountains of electronics being dumped there. Plus, the soil sample revealed high amounts of mercury and lead."

"What does that mean?" He eased back in his chair, as if it was taking time to absorb all that I just told him.

"It could mean some of these materials are seeping into the ground water, I'm not sure."

He started shaking his head and rubbed his index finger under his chin. "Okay, that explains why this gentleman was making threats."

"What? He made threats?" I couldn't believe my ears. Gil instantly went from weirdo to total psycho in my book.

"I won't get into the specifics, but I want you to stay away from the landfill and anything you are doing with this. You are too young to get involved. It's best to leave it up to the authorities."

"But this could be harming the people who live nearby," I moaned.

"I understand that. But it could also harm you," he said firmly.

I frowned. "I'll stay out of it."

Cody bounded into the room again, but this time with our labrador retriever, Magic trotting behind him. He whined, "Dad, can I play more video games?"

"I think you've had enough. Why don't you help your mother with some chores?"

I got up and said, "Or at least do some homework for a change."

My father shot me a look as I slipped out of the room. I could easily have been punished for that remark. My parents don't tolerate 'smart alecs'. But I couldn't be bothered with my annoying brother or the threats from Gil. I needed to crack this case!

Jett Log: 08.00 hrs.

As we drove to school the next day, my computer gave Julie an array of data, from air temperature to the percentage of clean air versus pollutants, to the tally of trash scattered along the road.

I could feel Julie's excitement when we passed the school bus and she glanced up to see everyone peering down at her.

"Feels good to have them admire you, doesn't it?" I asked.

"Sure does, Jett," she responded.

Minutes later we drove into the school parking lot. A few teachers had already arrived and were getting out of their cars. All eyes turned to Julie. Their cars were silent, sad, and old-fashioned compared to me. I wish I could have talked to them. They could have kept me company.

"Hi, Mrs. Farmer," Julie said, to a younger-looking teacher after she gave me the verbal command to "lock", which was our secret code word for "shut up." She made it up. How original.

"What a lucky girl you are," Mrs. Farmer said to Julie as she studied my form.

"Yes, I am very fortunate."

They walked toward the school and left me to rest. But I couldn't be too quiet; I'd need to keep an eye on Julie and her foes. I pulled up the computer network that runs the school and logged in. If anything should occur internally, I would have the chance to help out.

The V.O.T.

My mind buzzed with questions. Who was dumping the materials? Was money being made? How was I going to get a test of the water supply? Sounds of the classroom snapped me back, and I realized the metal chair I was sitting in was making my bottom go numb.

My environmental studies teacher, Mrs. North, exploded into the room. She whizzed by a pile of loose papers on her desk that fell to the floor. Without even a glance at the mess, her tiny mouth sprang to life. "It's V.O.T. time, folks! Let's prepare, shall we?"

The V.O.T. stood for the virtual oral test — the ultimate in testing terror. Each student had to go to a computer located at the front of the room and the teacher asked a series of questions. The answers were recorded electronically and recited out loud to the class. Because it was electronically administered, the teacher had the ability to change the questions, making them either difficult or easy. Each test was unique and made cheating nonexistent, or so we thought.

Mrs. North approached the computer monitor at the front of the room and switched it on. She then scurried through the rows of students to make sure everyone's own computer at their desk was working. Her high-pitched voice jangled my nerves as she explained the test and what percentage the grade counted toward year-end merits.

I keyed my password into the computer. A window popped up that showed the order each of us would be tested. The subject was climate change. I was third.

Pete leaned over to me and whispered, "Good luck."

"You too," I replied, as I nibbled on my stylus. I was worried that I wouldn't do well, since I had spent most of the previous night on a Web blog with environmentalists.

After the first two students had their turn, Mrs. North called on me. I wandered up to the screen at the front of the room. The first question was multiple choice; piece of cake.

I recited the second question that blinked on the screen. "At the end of the last Ice Age, much of the Northern Hemisphere was covered in ice. How did that affect the future make-up of the land?"

I swallowed hard. Luckily, I remembered the answer from a TV program I had recently watched. "It left the area as tundra, but thousands of years later it turned into forest," I said.

"Very good, Julie." Mrs. North lifted her fingers onto her keyboard and typed away.

The screen displayed a third question: Global warming could raise the sea level by how many inches by the end of the 21st Century?

I froze. I didn't know this one. The choices were 12 inches, 2 inches, 39 inches, and 60 inches. I guessed at 60 inches.

"Sorry Julie, that is incorrect," Mrs. North said. I had two more questions and then I was done.

I had gotten one wrong — not my typical style. Mrs. North grinned. "Nice effort, Julie."

I sat down. Pete took his turn and aced all of the answers. Then, it was Jonathan's turn.

Jonathan got up quickly and turned to the class smirking, like a clown. His first question was a multiple choice: Which animal has become extinct due to climate change? The choices were Golden Toad; Steel-eyed lizard; Panda; or Hyena. He tried to pick the Toad, but the button went to Hyena and didn't move. He tried clicking all the buttons and started slamming the mouse down, "I selected the toad," he shouted to the teacher.

"There is nothing wrong with the machine, Jonathan. Go to the next question, please," she said, tapping her fingers on the desk.

The next question asked him to explain what happened when the polar icecaps melted. He looked up from the screen and faced the class to explain the answer. Suddenly, the computer screen behind him switched to a picture of a polar bear sticking its tongue out. Everyone erupted in laughter, even Mrs. North. This made Jonathan stutter and lose his train of thought.

He faltered on the remaining questions and was

excused. I felt bad for him, but not too bad. *That Jett!* I thought.

Pete shot me a questioning look as I smiled over at him.

✳   ✳   ✳   ✳   ✳   ✳   ✳   ✳

After school, I strolled to the parking lot and jumped into Jett. I patted the front console. "Jett, did you plan on humiliating Jonathan?"

"I discovered that he was cheating and had all of the answers already programmed into his computer, so I had to set things straight."

I smiled and then got serious, "That's good, but there are more important things I need your help with," I said.

"What are they?" Jett asked eagerly.

"I need you to get the latest water test from the Regent Wells, and we need to go to the CHIPDOME. I have a hunch they might be involved with dumping electronics into the landfill."

Jett's hydrogen electric motor hummed to life. "You're on. Let's go!"

11

A Minor Detour

Our first stop after school was the CHIPDOME. On the way there, a car behind us flashed its headlights. I glanced in the computer monitor and did a double take. It was Gisele Nickels riding with some cute guy who was driving what looked like a brand new convertible. At first, I didn't know what to do.

Jett piped up. "Julie, I do believe someone wants your attention. I'd suggest a wave and a honk in reply."

"Oh, right. I must be dreaming," I said. I waved awkwardly. A honk ensued from the same direction.

"What do they want, Jett?" I whined.

"Relax, mate. I think the next logical step would be to pull over."

"Where?" I scanned the roadside, which was lined with trees.

"The CHIPDOME is the next driveway on your right."

Sure enough, the store was right around the corner. We signaled our entrance. They followed close behind.

"Breathe, Julie, you'll do fine," Jett said.

This was a day of firsts — I was taking advice from a car!

Gisele skipped toward the car. "I hope we didn't scare you," she chirped. Her blonde hair flowed out from under a broad-brimmed suede hat that coordinated with her outfit.

"Oh, not at all," I answered as I ran my fingers through my messy strawberry blonde hair.

Gisele gestured to the guy who had been driving and said, "Julie, this is my brother, Steve."

"Hi, Steve," I said tilting my head and trying not to stare. He stood nearly six feet tall and had dark brown hair, green eyes, and a muscular build.

"How did you get this amazing car?" he asked in a deep voice, his eyes locked on Jett.

"I entered a contest." I shifted nervously and pulled a strand of hair behind my ear.

Gisele looked at the car, then back at me. "I think it's way cool."

After a long pause, I spoke up. "Well, I hate to rush, but I need to check something out here and then get home for dinner."

"Oh yeah, dinner!" Gisele said with a hesitant smile. "That was the reason we stopped you to begin with, that and my brother wanted to check out your car. Would you like to come over to our house tomorrow night?"

My mouth opened wide, and I took a second to answer. "Uh, sure. Name a time, and I'll be there."

"How about six?" she asked.

"Perfect, I'll see you then. Ah, unless I see you at school first."

I waited patiently as they got back in their car and drove away. Whew! That was nerve-racking, I thought. I wasn't used to being approached by one of the coolest girls in the school. Everything was happening too fast — first Jett, then the landfill, the lab, and now this.

Inside the store, I walked straight down the center aisle. The shelves overflowed with electronic gizmos, from phones, to computers, to spy gear. I headed toward the back section, which was marked with a large blinking neon sign that said, "Service Here." A middle-aged, red-haired woman with glasses was stationed at the counter. She was wearing a bright yellow button that said, "Don't let the chips get you down! Power on UP today!"

She stopped chewing her gum and asked, "Yes, sweetie, may I help you?" Her southern drawl was distinct.

"Hi! I was wondering if you could tell me how I go about recycling my old computer?" I said in my most innocent schoolgirl voice.

"Love," she went on, snapping her gum against her teeth, "you'll need to speak with Neil Skid. He's our general manager. Hold on a sec, let me see if he is available." With that, she swiveled halfway around in her chair and whispered into the microphone attached to the headset she was wearing. Turning back to me, she said, "One moment, dearie, he just got off break."

As I waited, I noticed that all of the products were packed in boxes or in metal containers. The store had no fancy decor, no carpeting, just fluorescent lights and dust bunnies that had gathered on the hundreds of shelves and in corners of the store. After a few moments the general manager slithered out of the back room. Neil was a tall, skinny man with big hands and a receding hairline, and he was dressed head-to-toe in black leather.

"Can I be of assistance?" he asked in a raspy voice. I was distracted by the overwhelming smell of leather and a shiny necklace of the planet Saturn dangling from his neck. His leather pants squeaked when he moved. I hesitated and then asked, "Do you recycle old computers?"

"Why yes, we have a program with a company that comes by twice a week. Would you be interested?"

"How much money could I get?" I asked.

"It all depends on the model and age of your machine, but it usually averages anywhere from twenty to one hundred dollars," Neil replied.

"What company removes the equipment?"

"I'm not allowed to disclose that information," he said. "We do schedule pick-ups, if you want, but those are extra, of course."

"Okay, thanks for your help," I answered. "I'll call later." He handed me a flyer and I headed for the door.

I thought for a moment and remembered Jett's computer powers. "Jett, can you pull up the company that the CHIPDOME uses to recycle their equipment?" I requested.

"Sure, love," Jett replied, sounding just like the woman in the store. I smiled. He'd obviously been eavesdropping on their intercom system. He also could replicate human voices almost naturally. The computer buzzed into action. After a few seconds a message popped up on the screen: Unable to locate information.

"What does that mean?" I asked.

"It could be a glitch in the system, or it doesn't exist," he replied.

This seemed odd. "Can you keep trying?"

"Yes, I will keep scanning for that information. Any other requests?"

"No, that's it for now."

I glanced at the clock on the computer, and then groaned. "Oh no! I'm going to be late for dinner again." I tapped the audio button on the computer screen and called home.

12

Gracious Gisele

I had butterflies in my stomach as we drove up in front of Gisele's house. An electronic camera swiveled atop the iron gate as we stopped to be identified. Her house was set in a secluded hillside surrounded by woods. The quiet air was soon disturbed when a bevy of dogs started barking.

The gate swung open, and we drove toward the multi-level, Spanish-style house with decks overlooking the outdoor swimming pool and the valley below. After I parked Jett, I leapt out to see Gisele sitting in an enclosed porch on the side of the large modern home.

"Julie!" Gisele called out. "Come on up!"

I trotted up the steps, through the front door and took a sharp right. I flopped down on an overstuffed chair facing her and patted one of her dogs, a golden retriever, who was panting.

I smiled to myself. Gisele even matched her dog! She was dressed in a pair of gold pants that had a ribbon design woven throughout; her top was white and had tiny gold beads around the collar. Her long blonde hair was swept up on her head with a gold ribbon that matched her pants. She wasn't wearing shoes, which revealed her petite feet and toes that had been freshly painted a pale white. It made me realize how boring my clothes were. I was wearing a worn-out, light green long-sleeved shirt with washed out denim pants.

"I heard all about your e-studies class. How hilarious! I wish I'd been there," Gisele said with a grin.

"Seeing Jonathan squirm up in front of the class was the best." I laughed. "But I did feel a twinge of guilt."

"Why? You didn't make him screw up," she replied.

"Well, actually, I did, I mean my car and I did." I confessed.

"Really? That's so cool. But, he does deserve it. He's been bullying kids for years. And just to let you know, you aren't his only victim."

"Who else has he targeted?"

"Me, silly." She looked down at her feet and wiggled her toes.

"No way!" I said. "That's impossible. What did he have against you?"

"I was a threat to him being 'in'. I didn't like the way he treated one of my best friends. I had my brother Steve teach him a lesson."

"What did he do?" I asked, intrigued.

"He said he would start rumors about Jonathan being a 'daddy's boy' and a nerd if he continued to bother my friend."

The screen door flung open. "Gis, stop talking about me behind my back," Steve said, as he walked to the edge of the porch. He was wearing a short-sleeved shirt that showed off his tan and muscled arms.

"Hey, Julie, how are you?"

"Oh, I'm just fine," I answered. "Your sister and I were just discussing a mutual friend."

"Sounds like fun," Steve said, rolling his eyes. Turning to his sister, he said, "I'll be back soon. Dad needs me to pick up a package from a friend."

I watched, captivated, as Steve made his way down the stairs to the garage. Gisele caught me staring. "Your brother is very cute," I said shyly.

"Julie, I wouldn't get hung up on him. He's so intense with his acting and schoolwork that he hardly has time to sleep." The tone in her voice was authoritative, but I couldn't tell if it was a warning or a threat. Her voice changed to a softer tone. "So tell me, what do you do after school?"

I explained to her about my membership in E.V.E.N.. I briefly mentioned the landfill situation. I was a little nervous discussing this with her because I figured she wouldn't be that interested. Most people I met didn't particularly care about the environment. But to my surprise, she replied, "I've heard of E.V.E.N.. Can anyone become a member?"

"Sure, you just have to pass a test, go to meetings, and donate service hours to stay active."

"Tell me about some of the things you get to do."

"Let's see. We've stopped major companies from construction in fragile areas such as wetlands and forests. I helped plan and raise money for the annual Otterfest, a celebration of the otter that we saved from extinction. Then, there was the time Pete and I went hang-gliding to view damage from a forest fire. I could go on and on."

"Oooh, that sounds exciting," she purred. "You'll have to help me become a member."

The sound of tires on the gravel alerted all of the dogs, and a chorus of barking erupted.

"Sounds like my Dad's home. I hardly ever see him." Gisele said.

"That's like my Mom. She owns her own dental practice. I'm lucky I even see her at breakfast."

I fell silent as Mr. Nickels, Gisele's father, wandered onto the porch. He was an attractive man, dressed in a tailored suit with a brilliant scarlet colored tie. This contrasted with his blonde hair and wire-rimmed glasses. The strong scent of his cologne hung in the air.

"Who's this stranger talking with my beautiful daughter?" he bellowed.

"Hi, Dad," Gisele said. "This is Julie; we go to school together."

"A pleasure meeting you. Is that your car parked out front?"

"Yes, it is."

"It looks very New Age," he commented.

"It's an eco-advanced vehicle that I won in an essay contest," I said.

"Congratulations. That sounds exciting. What are you planning to do with it?" He approached my chair and his cologne became intoxicating.

"I'm working on a research project with the local landfill."

"Dad," Gisele chimed in, "before I forget, there's a message on the machine from your friend."

He walked over to Gisele and kissed her on the head. "Thanks, Angel," he said. I got the sense that her interruption upset him.

"It's time to eat," Gisele's mother announced as she poked her head around the screen door.

In the oval dining room, I admired how beautiful the table looked. It was set with silverware, fancy napkins, and numerous ornate candles. Everyone's plate was filled with a gourmet chicken dish, fresh steamed vegetables, and roasted potatoes. I sat across from Gisele. Steve, who had magically appeared from his journey, sat to my right, and her parents took each end of the oak table.

Gisele's father, after giving his wife rave reviews about the food, turned to me and asked, "What's this again about the local landfill?"

"It looks like there's been illegal dumping of electronic equipment," I answered.

"Do you know who is responsible?"

I shrugged. "The owner's name is Mr. Avalon. I've never met him, but I assume he has something to do with it."

"I hear he spends most of his time in Las Vegas gambling," Mr. Nickels said.

"I wasn't aware of that." I was surprised.

"Have you contacted him about this dumping problem?"

I was just about to answer when Gisele broke out

laughing. "Daddy, leave Julie alone. I'm sure she'd rather talk about saving the spotted owl or holding a recycling campaign."

"Actually, we've done all that, as I mentioned," I said, "but the landfill is a very serious issue." I looked back at Mr. Nickels who had a hard expression on his face.

He straightened up in his chair, leaned forward, and said gruffly, "Why don't the manufacturers take responsibility for this problem? I'm sure thousands of people don't obey the electronics disposal law."

"Father, what's your point?" Gisele asked, twirling her fork on her plate.

"My point is that most people are too busy with their jobs and families to worry about this," he said flatly.

I shot back at him, "Keep in mind, Mr. Nickels, that if certain chemicals get into our drinking water, then people's health will be affected, and then we'll all need to worry."

There was a long pause in the conversation until the shrill of a phone broke the silence. Mr. Nickels excused himself from the table to answer it.

Gisele's mother shifted nervously in her chair and asked, "Julie, how do you have time for this with school?"

"It's something I really care about, so I make time." Little did she know that lately I hadn't been exactly studying schoolwork.

"Glad to see I'm not the only one who is busy," Steve said as he passed the salt shaker to his sister.

I saw my chance and asked, "Will you excuse me?

I need to use the ladies room."

"It's down the hall next to the study," Mrs. Nickels instructed. This I knew from surveying the house when I first came in.

I walked softly down the hall and found the bathroom. I closed the door and waited. I really didn't need to use the room; I just wanted to hear Mr. Nickels' conversation. Something was up; he'd seemed agitated about the landfill problem, even more so when Gisele started interrupting him. I heard a muffled voice through the wall. I kneeled over the air vent on the floor, hoping that would give more clarity.

"I told you to be more careful!" Mr. Nickels said firmly, followed by the sound of the phone clicking off.

Then silence. Darn! I'd missed the entire conversation. I quickly turned on the faucet to wash my hands.

As I returned to the dining room, Gisele blurted, "Julie, do you want to go rafting with us this weekend?"

"Sure, that sounds like fun," I replied, pleased.

After we chatted about school and world topics for over an hour, I checked my watch and said, "I hate to have to leave, but it's getting late. Thanks again for dinner."

"Okay, I'll walk you to the door," Gisele said as she stood up to get my coat.

I walked outside into the cool night and glanced up at the stars. The Big Dipper and the Little Dipper were crystal clear. If only this case was.

I closed the car door tightly and turned on Jett. "Hey buddy, any information on the water sample or the CHIPDOME?" I asked.

"Ah, Julie. How are you, mate? Was the chicken too dry?"

"What? How did you know we had chicken?"

"A computer, love, operates the oven. It was set for poultry, and was on a little too long. I know things through the information I'm given."

I shook my head. "You know way too much."

"I haven't had a chance to crack the state's computers to find the water sample. But while you were chewing your dinner, I came across some interesting documents on Mr. Nickels' system."

"Excellent, what did you find?"

"He has made a few inquiries with the CHIPDOME recently."

"What type of inquiries?"

"How many computers are recycled on a weekly, monthly, and yearly basis."

"That seems fishy. Why would he care?" I lifted my hand off the steering wheel, letting Jett navigate.

"There was one other thing I discovered."

"Which was?"

"He was accessing secure files about cars similar to me."

13

The Recycle Council

The cell phone screamed in my ear. I reached frantically out from under my pillow and grabbed it. My voice was rough. "Ah, hello?"

"Julie!" Pete yelled. "Wake up! Today's the meeting of the Recycle Council and Meredith is making an announcement!"

I rubbed my eyes and said, "Oh shoot, I forgot to set my alarm." What a drag, I just wanted to sleep.

"Can you pick me up in an hour?" he demanded.

"I'll be there." I hung up and suddenly remembered that today I was going to be with Gisele and Steve again. My stomach stirred with excitement.

I heard a knock at the door. It had that parent rhythm to it, not too loud, but consistent and firm. "Come in," I called.

"Sorry to wake you this early," said my mother. She was wearing a pair of jeans and a sweater with a tag hanging from the sleeve. Which was odd, since she never wore jeans and she hardly had time to buy anything new, much less food.

"You look great. I like the outfit," I commented as I pulled the covers up around my shoulders.

"Why, thanks." She sat at the end of my bed and looked at me with concern. "Is everything alright with you?"

I nodded. "Yes, why do you ask?"

"Cody mentioned that some boy at school was giving you a hard time about the car."

I sighed. "Oh, that. That's old news. And besides, he hasn't bugged me in awhile."

"But do you feel safe?"

"Now that I have Jett, I feel much safer. We're a team." I patted her hand. "Please don't worry, Mom."

"I know your father talked with you about the threat," she said, "I hope you realize how serious this is."

"Yes, I do." What was up with her? That was days ago. She reminded me of the relief pitcher in our family; she understood the game, but when she stayed out too long, she got rusty.

We discussed the day and her agenda. Everything in her world had to be planned. After she left, I wandered over to my computer. A button on the screen was flashing. What was this? I clicked on it, and it displayed the records of the past monthly well inspections at the landfill. I scrolled through page after page of detailed reports. All of the tests came up negative for toxic materials.

I clicked on the voice-activation signal on the computer to Jett. I burst out, "This can't be right! I know there's got to be some water damage from the dumping. What do you think, Jett?"

"The lab computers might have something to do with this."

"What do you mean?"

If one hacker can tap into those, what makes you think he'd stay away from these?"

"Yes, of course, it could definitely be the same person. I'm coming down. We have a meeting to go to."

I quickly got dressed and flew down the stairs. I scanned the spotless kitchen and realized I'd missed fast break. I grabbed an apple and tiptoed across the hallway to the front door to avoid my brother, who was usually in the den.

"Hey, pest," Cody shrieked. "Where are you going?"

"None of your business," I replied, facing the door.

"You'd be nicer to me if you knew what I did."

"What do you know that I don't?" I asked as I swung my head around.

"Jonathan found out that you set him up in class."

I stopped. "Who told you that?"

"The word is out, he wants revenge."

"Thanks for the warning," I said, annoyed. He shrugged and continued playing his video game.

On the drive to Pete's, I alerted Jett to my brother's warning about Jonathan and that I mentioned it to Gisele. She's the only one who knew we were behind it. Why would she do that? I was confused. I thought she was on my side. Jett replied by saying not to worry about it and that he'd keep an eye on her.

We pulled up in front of the ranch-style home where Pete lived. The house looked old and was in desperate need of a paint job. Pete and his mother lived alone. His father had left when he was a baby, and his mother worked full-time as a nurse to support them.

I honked the horn, and Pete bounded out of the garage. His hair was wet, as if he had just gotten out of the shower, and he was wearing unlaced hiking boots, jeans, and a faded safari shirt.

"Hi," I said as he plopped down in the passenger seat.

"Good morning!" he said.

"You look like you're ready to go to a Hawaiian luau."

"It still feels like summer, and I wanted to take advantage of it."

"Who's coming today?"

"Tim, Zane, and Jones are planning on being there, and of course, Meredith. It will be the six of us. The meeting of the minds."

As we drove along, the sun started to peek through the clouds. I instructed Jett to open the solar sunroof by saying, "Open sun." The air felt warm on my skin. Jett reported the smog index was close to zero with a slight breeze coming out of the northeast.

"Turn here," Pete instructed. We drove down a gravel driveway that was lined with oversized pine trees. A farmhouse stood in the distance. It was ivory-colored with black shingles, a large front porch, and a second story deck.

We could also see the edges of a red brick barn behind the house. To the right of the house was a large corral. Suddenly, we heard a thundering sound and saw a spirited chestnut-colored horse come galloping along the fence line. The horse's ears were pricked forward and his nostrils flared as if excited by our presence.

"Looks like Prana is happy to see us!" Pete said.

My eyes grew wide with delight as the beautiful horse pranced along the fence, throwing his strong head up and down.

As soon as Jett parked, the front door opened and a miniature collie trotted out, followed by a slight woman. Her long wavy auburn hair cascaded beneath the cowboy hat she always wore.

"Well, if it isn't the double trouble twins!" she called in a deep husky voice, trying to be heard over her dog.

"Hi, Meredith!" I said.

"Julie, you must tell me all about this fancy car." She tapped her fingers on Jett's hood. Then her gaze turned to Pete. "Oh, Pete, you are looking thinner than ever. Don't you eat?"

"Yes, but I've been busy at school."

"You need to relax. Plenty of time for that when you get older."

"Is everyone here?" I asked.

"Just about. We're waiting on Jones to arrive by helicopter. He was out in the field doing research on forest fires early this morning. Come on; let's go inside with Tim and Zane."

Meredith proceeded to the door as her collie, Shady, whisked by. Looking at her walk easily, I recalled that it was a miracle Meredith was alive today.

When Meredith was only five years old, she swam in a contaminated lake without knowing it. A few days later she started having flu-like symptoms and problems breathing. Her condition went from bad to worse, even with antibiotic treatment. Luckily, the chief doctor was an environmentalist and had been studying ways to clean water for years. He knew of only one cure, and it was no guarantee. He used an herbal supplement powered with a bioengineered protein and, within days, Meredith started to feel better. Her appetite and strength slowly came back. After one week, Meredith was on her feet looking for ice cream in the hospital's refrigerator.

From that day on, Meredith devoted herself to cleaning up the environment and studying the effects it had on humans. She traveled the world helping spread the word and provided assistance on solving various countries' environmental problems.

We walked into the cozy farmhouse to find Tim and Zane playing a game of virtual chess. Tim and Zane were identical twins, and we always had trouble figuring out who was who. They were of Chinese descent and had fair skin, almond-shaped brown eyes, and cropped black hair. Luckily, they wore baseball caps from their favorite Digital Express League teams. Tim was a Tronics fan, and Zane was devoted to the Laser Lights. The league featured computer-animated players in a sport that resembled hockey but was played more like football.

"Hi, guys, are you having fun?" I asked. Both of them continued playing chess deep in concentration.

A few seconds later, Tim grunted. "Yeah, barely."

"Tim, you are such a sore loser," said Zane. He turned to us, his brow looked tense. "Don't you worry, I'll knock him out in a minute, and then we'll be all yours!"

I looked back near the kitchen and saw Meredith beckoning to me. "A minute equals an hour in chess time," she said. "Come here and help me carry these." She pointed to a plate of snacks.

I heard the roar of the helicopter blades cutting the air in the distance and growing more intense as it got closer.

"Looks like Jones could join us," Meredith said, glancing out the window.

Pete went over and observed the game board. He shook his head. "Zane, I guess I shouldn't doubt you. You are winning!"

Shady started barking when the helicopter landed. Shortly after, there was a loud knock at the door.

Without hesitation, Jones came bounding in. He was over six feet tall, with a lean build, short black hair, and a week-old beard coming in.

"Hey brothers and sisters! Sorry I took this long. The Lord abetted my quick release," Jones said. He was always quoting God as if they traveled together as friends.

"We were just getting settled. You have perfect timing." Meredith replied.

Everyone took a seat in the living room.

Meredith cleared her throat and said, "We received some news from the Washington D.C. office today that a new lethal powder may become available on the market. The reason they are alerting environmental groups is because there is a link between electronics and the hazardous substances in them that are used to make this powder. This is speculative and is in the early stages of investigation. If anyone has information on this, please let me know."

"What can this so-called powder do?" Zane asked.

"It is believed to have the power to blow up a large city, or, if used correctly, it could power a space shuttle."

"Does anyone else have any other important news?"

I raised my hand and told everyone the details of my landfill search and the results of the testing.

Tim smoothed his hat. "Do you consider this a code E?"

"Not yet, but it could get to that stage." A code E was a call for emergency level assistance and involved more than just the six of us. It meant we had to report the problem to the authorities, and the national E.V.E.N. agency would provide volunteers if needed.

The meeting was quickly adjourned. Tim and Zane resumed playing chess while Jones and Meredith chatted about their jobs.

"See you soon," Meredith said, as she opened the door to let us out.

Jett Log: 12.30 hrs.

That's my girl, getting the team involved. Talk about a serious case of who's up to no good. I'll need to do some investigating on this lethal powder issue. I have a hunch the landfill has something to do with it. Let's see if Julie can find out any information from her two new friends.

14

More Than One Mountain

Gisele had her hands on her hips and paced in a small circle. She glanced at her watch and whined, "Julie, you are almost an hour late. What took you so long?"

After the meeting, I had to drop off Pete at his house and change clothes. It took me longer than I anticipated. "Sorry, I had some chores to do first."

She swung her ponytail and marched toward Steve who was organizing the gear and cleaning the rubber raft. I followed a few steps behind. As we got closer I waved apologetically and said, "Hey, I'm finally here. Can I help?"

"All set," Steve said as he clipped his safety harness to his orange life vest. "Julie, you'll need to follow our instructions since you're a beginner. As the guide, I'll steer and sit in the back of the raft. You'll be in the center, and Gisele will be up front. If you have any problems, you'll need to holler. It gets pretty loud out there."

I observed the shallow, blue river and noticed the flow was calm.

The sound of the water gurgled over the stones.

I asked, "Are we actually going to get anywhere in these so-called rapids?"

"Relax," Steve answered. "The fall typically produces slower rapids than spring, and besides, this is only a launch area. You'll see how soon it picks up."

We all grabbed the lightweight raft and slipped it into the water. Steve helped us onboard by holding out his hand for support. He hoisted himself into the rear seat and dug the oar into the sandbank. It sent us midstream, and the current slowly lifted the raft along.

Gisele was sitting in front of me so that I was looking at her back. Click, click, click. She was adjusting her watch. I called, "What will that do?"

"It allows me to track our speed and time." Then she turned to me and said gruffly, "And by the way, you don't need to ask any more questions, because Steve and I have been doing this since we were little. Steve wins the 'raft master' award every year."

Steve responded quickly by adding, "Jules, don't let my sister get to you. She's just in a bad mood."

I sat quietly and turned my face to the north to feel the cool breeze. The river narrowed into an area with many trees lining the banks. I zipped up my temperature-activated pullover and took a deep breath, smelling the fragrant autumn leaves.

Suddenly Steve yelled, "Approaching rapids! Hold on, Julie, and take in your paddle. You won't need it right now."

Sure enough, our raft felt as if an invisible hand had picked us up and pushed us swiftly down a water chute.

The raft thrashed up and down so much I felt like I was on a bucking horse. At first, I was nervous, but then I relaxed and really got into it.

Steve and Gisele shouted back and forth, guiding each other about where the rocks were and how deep the drop might be. After some quick rapids, a patch of flat water appeared, and we paddled to a tiny island in the middle of the river to have some lunch. My stomach grumbled with hunger.

"Hey, junior rafter, are you having a good time?" Gisele asked with a slight smile.

"This is amazing, I love it!" I said between gulps of fortified bottled water.

"You looked a little nervous in the beginning, but I knew you would get the hang of it," Steve said.

I turned to Gisele and asked skeptically, "Are you feeling better?"

"Yeah, I just needed to be away from my dad. He can be a bit overbearing."

Steve opened up the food containers and announced, "Plenty of eats. Help yourself."

"Julie, tell us more details on how you won the car." Gisele said.

I briefly described my essay and my grandparent's farm. I explained how I came across the magazine and how many people had entered the contest.

"You had PJ give you a demonstration on how to use the car?" Gisele inquired.

"Well, yes." I hesitated. "But how did you know the engineer's name? I didn't mention that."

Her eyes flickered. "Oh, I thought you said his name. Maybe not, but lucky guess." She shrugged.

Steve cleared his throat. "Our father knows people in the automotive industry. I'm sure Gisele has heard him speak of PJ in the past. He's fairly well-known."

"What does your father actually do?" I asked them.

Steve and Gisele glanced at each other, and Gisele responded, "He's a lawyer who represents automotive companies."

"That explains why he was interested in Jett," I said out loud. It might also explain the documents Jett found on Mr. Nickels' computer. Could he have been just doing research for a client?

"Yes, it spurs his curiosity," said Gisele looking down at her plate.

Steve got to his feet and started to pack up the extra food. "I was thinking about taking another part of the river today. That okay with both of you?"

Gisele chirped, "That sounds like fun!"

After we got back into the raft, Steve pointed out a narrow part of the river that branched off to the right, as if it had sprouted an arm. "It's up ahead. Hard right, Gisele. Hold on, Julie!"

The river was calm for a few minutes, and then the water started building momentum. I admired the white birch trees as their branches bowed into the river. It looked like wooden fingers combing the current. Their yellow leaves shimmered as the soft breeze tangoed with the sunshine.

The raft bounced on as the river grew narrower,

sometimes getting so close that we had to be careful not to get caught up in the trees. Suddenly, something caught my eye. It glimmered on the bank, catching the sun, and at first I thought it was a leaf.

"Hey, you guys," I shouted. "Head for that object on the bank to the right about twenty feet ahead."

"What do you see, Julie?" Gisele asked.

"I'm not quite sure."

"Hold on, I'll get us there," she said, plunging her oar fiercely into the water.

As we swept by the object, I grabbed it. I whipped off some waterlogged leaves, and in my hands lay a circuit board from an old computer.

I gasped, "I can't believe this!"

"Wow! Where could that have come from?" Steve said. "We are at least ten miles from the nearest house."

"I have a suspicion we might be uncovering more of this. Let's keep going." I replied.

The raft edged slowly along the river.

"Why are we going so slowly?" Gisele asked.

"Maybe something is preventing the flow ahead of us," Steve said.

Sure enough, we hadn't traveled more than a hundred feet when we started seeing more pieces of computer equipment mixed in with debris from the river and caught in the branches of the overhanging trees. It appeared to be the makings of a dam, but an unnatural one.

"Steve," I called, "Can we turn around? I have a

hunch we're near a landfill and that is where this is coming from."

Steve swung the raft around with some muscle power from Gisele as well. After what seemed like an hour, we returned to the part of the river where we had taken a right turn. On the far side of it, beyond the fork in the river, I could make out the beginning of the working face of a landfill.

I pointed. "Straight ahead. I'm pretty sure that is where it's coming from!"

As the rapids merged, it made it extremely difficult to get to the other side.

"Steve, I need more paddle on the left!" Gisele yelled. "I'm losing my headway."

"I just need to get my paddle on a rock to give us some stability. Hold on!"

I heard Steve frantically dipping the paddle into the water, but there was no sound of his paddle against a rock.

"Steeeeve, hurry up!" Gisele sounded frantic.

"Is there anything I can do?" I shouted. The sound of the rapids filled my head, and I didn't hear a response from either one of them. I noticed that the raft was taking on water, which affected our ability to maneuver quickly.

I shut my eyes for a minute as the water splashed on me. When I opened them, we had miraculously started moving to the other side of the river. As we got close to the bank, we all grabbed onto low-lying shrubs to help pull ourselves up.

Once we had dragged the raft up on the bank, Steve and Gisele lay down in the grass, breathing heavily.

"Stay here! I'm going to investigate. I'll be back in a few minutes," I said.

I managed to undo my waterproof vest and get out my digital camera. I started running to the landfill. In minutes, I reached the perimeter fence. There, behind the chain link fence, were mountains of old computer equipment.

I started taking photos and recorded my position to Jett on the camera's 'text messaging' feature. I scanned the border and noticed that one of the fence poles was sticking out, allowing for slack on the chain link. I pulled on the pole to loosen it more and crawled under the links.

Once I was inside, I frantically circled the mounds of waste, careful not to fall on any sharp objects. I knew I needed help on this one. Using my camera I sent another signal to Jett. I needed the car to do a search and scan through my camera lens for anything suspicious.

Jett sent me a location to check out on my watch. Sure enough, he'd spotted a large white box with the name CHIPDOME stamped on the side. Inside, there were pieces of a computer and a recycling receipt with the signature of Neil Skids, the manager of CHIPDOME.

"Save these images, Jett," I instructed. Then crawled back through the opening and ran down the hill to Steve and Gisele.

"Miss Environment, can we get a move on?" Steve shouted when he saw me.

"Sorry, I'm making a habit of being late today. But thanks for letting me explore."

"Can we get out of this stinking place now?" Gisele pinched her nose.

"Hurry up," Steve said as he watched the sun setting. "Let's get back into the raft and get to our cars. I didn't plan for this to be an overnight."

Luckily, our ride down the river was smooth and quiet. We were all tired by the time we made it back to where the cars were parked. I kept what I found a secret from them. Too much was riding on this, and I couldn't afford to let anyone know. Plus, I wasn't buying Gisele and Steve's story that they heard of PJ from their father's line of work.

"I have good news, Julie," Jett said to me, as we drove home. "While you went running off with your new pals, I tapped into the inspection office that contains the files for all of the state's landfills. This includes all of the well tests."

"What did you find?"

"The Regent Landfill was approved last week."

I sighed and shook my head. "That's not good news."

"But wait, I also uncovered that someone tampered with the records."

"You're positive?"

"Yes, I'm sure. The code name was 'bunker01'. Do you have any idea what that stands for?"

"A bunker is a sand trap in golf. The only golfer

I know is Gil," I said.

"The same ID appears with the person who tried to crash the system at the E.V.E.N. agency," Jett added.

"I think it's time we paid another visit to the landfill," I said.

"I recommend we try the CHIPDOME first," Jett replied. "Trust me on this one."

Print Worthy

I peered through the glass window marked 'News' to see Pete sitting on a chair facing the school courtyard below. It looked as if he was an eagle sitting on a perch. Early morning was his favorite time of day. He said it was good for finishing up any last minute stories before the nine o'clock deadline, and it gave him time to think of new ones. His Journalism teacher had given him a key to the room since he was the editor of the "The Atlas."

I knocked on the door softly, hoping not to startle him. He turned around and looked at me with a hesitant smile. He gestured for me to come in.

"Hi there," I said. I hadn't seen him since the meeting, and he seemed distant.

"What brings you by on a Monday morning this early?"

"I have some interesting news," I said, crossing the floor to sit by him near the window. "When I went rafting yesterday we came upon a second landfill that had mounds of electronics piled up and was also causing a dam in the river." I paused to watch his eyes widen with surprise and added, "I even found a receipt in the landfill with Neil Skid's name on it."

"So much for their recycling program. Do you know why this is happening?"

"That's why I'm here. I need your help."

His face lit up. "Ah, I'm at your service."

"I need you to research anything and everything about the Regent Landfill. And we need to call another council meeting."

"Great minds think alike, come see what I was doing before you arrived." He clicked on a story that focused on how the school trash was recycled. It included a picture of the landfill with Gil standing in front of the perimeter fence. He read out loud, "Gil has received extensive training in computer science for projects he completed at his past job, where he handled the security and inspection of a government agency."

"Which makes it no surprise that he knows how to tamper with well records," I said.

Pete nodded and ran his fingers through his messy hair. "There was one other piece of information that I came across in researching my article that I wanted to share with you."

Suddenly, we heard the clicking of heels coming down the hallway. Pete looked up from the computer and said, "Quick! Get in the closet. My teacher doesn't like it when I have people in here before school starts."

I ran into the storage closet and closed the door. Tiny slats in the door allowed me to see out, but made it nearly impossible to see in.

There was a faint knock. "Come in," Pete called.

In walked Gisele. She had her blonde hair pulled back and was wearing colorful, stylish pants with a top that had embroidered designs down the sleeves. Her eyes sparkled with mystery as she looked at him.

"Pete, I'm glad you are here. I have a story idea for you," she said quietly.

"Shoot. What is it?"

"My father is building a space museum and the grand opening is at the end of the month," she said.

"That sounds exciting. Would he let me interview him?" he asked.

"Sure, I'll see what I can do." She looked a bit uneasy as her eyes darted from him to the window.

"Did you see Julie at all yesterday?"

"No, I was busy with homework and writing." Pete's eyes narrowed. "Weren't you with her on Saturday?"

"Yes. She left behind some clothing in the raft, and I wanted to give it to her," she said and walked over to the door. She looked at the floor and said, "You know, we had fun the other day. You should join us sometime."

"Ah, sure, that would be great," Pete said dubiously.

I knew how awkward Pete must have been feeling.

Gisele swiftly left the room. As soon as I heard the door close, I burst out of the closet. "That was weird. Seemed like she basically wanted to find out if I was around yesterday."

Pete started pacing back and forth. "The space museum opening is common knowledge, but I didn't realize how involved her father is. In the press releases, they always mention a development company."

"Something doesn't add up," I said.

"Isn't her father a lawyer for a car company?" Pete asked.

I nodded. "But remember what Jett discovered when I was having dinner at Gisele's? Her father's computer system had entries to the CHIPDOME."

"And doesn't Neil have a fondness for space?"

"That might explain who Mr. Nickels was talking with the night I had dinner there."

"Wow! And I thought the lead of Gil's was print worthy!"

"What was that other thing you wanted to share with me?"

"I recently came across an article about new experiments that NASA is working on with recycled electronics, but in order to gain more information, I needed a secure government approved I.D."

"That could be the missing piece that we need to nab our landfill menace. If you uncover anything else, just let me know."

"Right. And Julie, be careful!" Pete gave me an awkward hug.

16

Cool Girl

I was standing in front of my locker retrieving my lunch when I heard Gisele's distinct giggle directly behind me.

"Jules, your locker looks too neat. I've never seen a locker you could actually find things in."

I felt my face flush as I turned around to face her. "It's just easier that way," I replied. I had managed to snatch my lunch container and clutched my book bag in my other hand.

"Why don't you join me and my friends for lunch?" she asked.

I immediately thought about that morning. Here was my chance to see how truthful or conniving she was. Gisele would have to pass my little test. Pete would understand.

"Sure, that would be nice," I replied.

We walked down the hall together, and I couldn't help but feel the attention that she attracted. People would wave to her and she'd smile or give a slight wave back. Even the teachers acknowledged her. I received a few looks — I think more of shock than acceptance. We reached the crowded cafeteria with its rows of round tables and bright banners advertising an upcoming school play. The room was split up by grade level and marked distinctly by the color table you sat at. Our ninth grader tables were blue.

Gisele had to buy her lunch, so she escorted me to her usual table. There were six of her friends already there. She introduced them to me, including Cindy, who a week ago wouldn't have given me the time of day. Gisele smoothed her tight-fitting blouse and announced, "Take care of Julie while I'm gone, ladies." With that, she turned and disappeared into the sea of students waiting in line for food.

I slid into one of the chairs between Cindy and Samantha. They gave me a quick smile and continued discussing a serious issue: their favorite lipstick and color.

A few seconds later, Cindy turned to me and asked, "Julie, what brand do you wear?" She immediately broke out laughing and said, "Oh, that's right, you don't wear any makeup. You're into the natural look."

I tried not to let this bother me and replied, "You didn't know that the natural look was in this year? I guess I'm just a trend-setter." They all laughed at this and quickly moved onto another topic.

I finished my yogurt and one of the girls started pointing behind me. I could feel someone standing near me. As I turned around, my mouth dropped. Pete was standing there with his bag lunch, which had leaked through and was dripping down his pant leg. Why me? This was completely embarrassing. Before I could say anything, Gisele came bounding over.

"Pete, this is a girls-only table. Why don't you find your own table to sit at?" She wrinkled her nose as she looked at the mess on his pants. "Better yet, you might want to spend some time in the bathroom." A chorus of giggles broke out, and Pete's face drained. He turned on his heels and ran out of the cafeteria.

Gisele patted my shoulder. "Wow! Good thing I saved you from breaking the news to him about sitting with us."

I pretended to smile and ended up forcing food in my mouth to keep from screaming. I felt bad for Pete, but he should have known not to bother me at a table that was clearly all girls.

A warning bell sounded, signaling ten more minutes of the lunch period. Most of the girls got up to clear their trays, then headed to the bathroom for some pre-class primping.

Gisele stayed with me. "How's Jett?" she asked. She frowned with concern. "Did you ever think about what would happen if your car got stolen?"

"Jett is smart enough to know what is happening around him and has the resources to protect himself," I said. It was about time to see what Gisele was really up to, so I slipped in the bait. "Also, the engineer who designed the car gave me this." I reached into my book bag and pulled out a random disk. "It shuts down the entire system."

She stared and said, "That's amazing. Sounds like he thought of everything. But why would you need to shut it down?"

I hesitated. "Oh, he mentioned something about the computer controlling something, I wasn't really sure."

The next bell sounded, so I put the disk back in the side pocket of my book bag and got up to leave.

"Why don't we go to the bathroom quickly before class?" Gisele offered.

I agreed, and we set off in the direction of the nearest bathroom. Inside, Gisele asked, "Do you have a brush I could borrow?"

"Sure, it's in my bag," I answered and then walked into the first stall, knowing her plan.

When I came out Gisele was zipping up my bag. "Thanks, I look much better," she said, as we headed to class.

"Gisele, thanks for inviting me to lunch," I told her. "I had a nice time."

"You're welcome, cool girl. Anytime." She grinned and immediately turned to say hello to a hockey player.

Ah, it seemed like a whole new world walking in her shoes. After she had gone into class, I unzipped the pocket — no disc. Suddenly I realized the impact of her action in the girl's room. She could not be trusted.

17

The Map

The following Saturday the sharp sound of thunder woke me instantly and shook the whole house as it rolled through the valley. It was no use going back to sleep since I had planned on going to the CHIPDOME early before the Recycle Council meeting.

After a quick breakfast, I dressed and hurried out the door. As I ran to the garage, large pellets of rain began to fall. I gasped as I opened the door to the garage. Jett was now disguised as a truck. Since Gisele clearly wanted something from Jett, I decided to bring him to P.O.D.D.S (Port of Detachable Devices Station) to change his bodywork. I told my parents that we were doing a project with E.V.E.N. to clear out brush in the woods and we needed a truck to haul it away. It took the entire day, but by the time I came back from school, the sleek, sporty Jett was now a two-door, long-bed, cherry red pick-up truck. I was still getting used to it, and I could tell by the tone in his voice that Jett wasn't too happy with his new look.

At the store I pulled behind a row of parked cars. Since Neil had already met me, I felt having a disguise would be wise. I was wearing a black wig and black-framed glasses. A coat of cotton-candy pink lipstick covered my lips. I smiled. Gisele would have loved it. As I entered the store, I noticed posters everywhere. The CHIPDOME 3rd Annual Fall Carnival was being held in the parking lot tomorrow.

My mission was to get into Neil's office and place a "memory-reader" on the back of his computer. This is a tiny chip that would allow Jett to access all of the files in order to trace history and current activity. I needed to prove that they tampered with the well records and see if Neil was responsible for the illegal dumping.

Jett had given me a map of the store, so I knew exactly which office belonged to the store manager. The door was wide open. I looked around to make sure no one was paying attention, then slipped in and attached the memory-reader to his computer. The office was cluttered and filled with papers and pictures of planets and space objects.

I took a digital photo of the office for my files. My arm briefly glazed the mouse pad and suddenly it exposed a hidden compartment below. A map of what looked like a museum was lying there. Intrigued, I grabbed it and ran.

As I walked briskly down one of the aisles, I could hear a voice calling out behind me. "Miss? Miss? Where were you..."

The automatic doors opened and I dashed out.

That afternoon we all gathered at the E.V.E.N. lab. Pete hadn't returned my phone calls after the cafeteria incident, so I went alone.

As I walked in, everyone's eyes were on me.

Meredith approached me first, "Julie, I think it's time we set up a plan to confront the landfill villains."

Jones immediately wrapped his arm around my shoulder and pulled me close to him. "We'll get this done with God's help and my trusty helicopter."

"Tell us about the map you found at the CHIPDOME," Tim said.

"It is of the space museum."

"Don't you think Neil will be looking for it?"

"Yes. That's why we need to act soon before he finds out."

"We have the carnival tomorrow, won't that be the best time to catch these fellows?" Meredith inquired, her face tense.

"That was exactly what I was thinking."

"Why the carnival?" Jones asked.

"It's a perfect diversion," I answered.

"And who's going to be the diversion?" He grinned.

"That's where you guys come in. I need your help to think of what would make the most sense." I sat down and looked at each of them.

Tim scratched his head and announced, "I've got it! We have the hot air balloon rides scheduled at the same time the CHIPDOME truck comes to log in the recycled computers. Everyone will be busy watching us. This will give you a chance to follow them to one of the landfills."

"I like it!" I said. "Since we need to catch them in the act of dumping the so-called recycled computers."

"What happens if we have trouble following them?" Jones asked. "We'll schedule a pick-up and have the computer traceable."

"Is that possible?" Meredith's tension had changed to excitement.

"Sure, I'll have my brother, Cody do it," I answered. "And then what?"

Jones paced back and forth, his boots leaving an imprint on the carpet. He mumbled to himself, then said, "Yes, this could work! First, we trace the computer. The driver will stop at the CHIPDOME to check in and collect more materials before they deposit them in the 'fill. Julie and Jett can follow them to get photos of the dumping in action. Then, I'll fly the helicopter to make sure everything is running smoothly. Voila!"

"Wait a minute, how do we know they are going to dump tomorrow?" Zane asked.

"I've attached a tracer on Neil's computer and we discovered the next one is scheduled for tomorrow," I replied.

"But what if Neil decides it's too risky?"

"We can have Jett disguise his voice as Gil to force him to carry out the instructions," I replied.

"Ok, it's a plan," Meredith said. "Everyone set on their duties?"

We nodded in unison.

18

Carnival

At one o'clock sharp Cody placed the phone call to the CHIPDOME to have his computer removed for recycling. Jett and I waited down the block for the pick-up to take place. Within thirty minutes, a beat-up looking silver van pulled into our driveway. Two men in beige shirts, that had CHIPDOME embroidered on their sleeves, brought a cart with them up to the door.

Cody opened the door and greeted them.

"Hi there, boy," one of the men said, looking down at Cody, who was wearing a pair of shorts and a juice-stained T-shirt.

"The computer is right here in the hall," he said politely to the driver.

The two men loaded the computer onto the cart. Cody scribbled his signature, and the men gave him a receipt for his records. Then they transferred the cart and computer to the van. As soon as they pulled out of the driveway, Cody gave me the 'thumbs up' and we prepared to follow them. Their van lurched forward like a bee leaving its hive, traveling straight and fast. Jett and I stayed a couple hundred feet behind.

The van raced along the country roads heading

toward the CHIPDOME. As we pulled up to the entrance it was as if an explosion of color, noise, and heat had descended on the entire place. I had never seen that many people packed into a parking lot the size of a football field. Small tents were snuggled up under the giant rides, and the air was thick with the smell of buttery popcorn, cotton candy, and greasy hot dogs fresh off the fryer.

The van slowed to a crawl trying to make its way to the loading dock behind the store. The entire area was teeming with people trying to get to and from their parked cars.

I jumped out of Jett to take pictures of the van in the loading dock area. Across the parking lot, I saw a large shadow. I immediately looked up and saw a hot air balloon descending over the crowd and heading towards a grassy area. The balloon's outer shell had a bright yellow and blue stripe with a picture of a bird on one side that represented the E.V.E.N. insignia. The balloon rides were a big hit with the locals.

The two men who had picked up the computer disappeared through a set of double doors and minutes later emerged with a cart of a dozen used computers. I grabbed my digital camera to take pictures while they threw the goods into the van. "Hey!" Suddenly my camera was ripped from my hands. Standing before me was Jonathan.

A huge smile spread across his face. "Julie, you really think you'll get away with this?"

"Jonathan, if you only knew what was going on,

you'd think twice about taking my camera," I said with a sigh.

"It's about time you paid for humiliating me during e-studies," Jonathan said.

How did I know that would come back to haunt me?

"Hey, give me that back!" This was going to ruin our plans. I suddenly remembered that Gisele said that Jonathan was a total wimp with his father. "Oh, look over there. Isn't that your father?" I screeched.

His head spun around, as he started scanning the crowd. I took my chance, and turned to run toward the hot air balloon. I ran as fast as I could, my legs straining to build up speed. I could hear Jonathan running behind me as people started yelling at him. "Hey, watch it, you big freak," one woman cried out.

Tim was holding the basket of the hot air balloon, getting it ready for the next ride. I shouted out to him, "Let me go up next! Jonathan is chasing me!"

Tim nodded and opened the basket for me. As I got in, he jumped in as well and turned the burners on to fuel the hot air. This powered the balloon upwards.

Unfortunately, the balloon was too slow to come off the ground. We both stared as Jonathan emerged from the crowd. He was running at full speed toward us.

I looked at Tim and moaned, "I think he's going to try and jump in. What can we do?"

Before Tim could answer, Jonathan lunged over the top of the basket and landed hard. The basket swung violently back and forth from the weight of the impact.

Tim and I grabbed onto the outer ropes to brace us from falling.

I screamed at Tim, "Get us down!" I could feel the balloon steady and climb upwards. I was now petrified for two reasons. One, I was afraid of heights and two, I was with my archenemy.

"Relax. I just need to shut the burner off and pull the valve rope to let the air out of the top, and we should be down in a minute," he said. Jonathan was rubbing his head. Tim pulled forcefully on the rope, but suddenly half of the rope snapped off. Tim's eyes went wide with panic while holding the other half of the rope. "Julie, it looks like someone wanted this to happen. The rope was three quarters of the way severed already."

Then, we heard sobbing coming from Jonathan. Tears were streaming down his face. I asked gruffly, "What is your problem, cry baby? You got us into this mess!"

He managed to reply, "I'm scared of heights."

I momentarily forgot I was scared as well and knew I had to hide it anyway. "You should have thought of that when you jumped in after me."

He shrugged and looked away, shaking with terror.

I bit down on my lip and suddenly realized the danger we were in.

Jett Log: 11.00 hrs.

If only kids these days would think. Why did she run off to the balloon when she could have just hopped back into me? Unbelievable! Now she'd been whisked away in an ancient flying contraption. Some inventor sure wasn't thinking clearly when he came up with air travel in an oversized balloon. Talk about taking your time to get from one place to the next.

The timing of her mishap couldn't have been worse. It was almost time for the delivery to go out — the one we were planning on following. Now I had to worry about Julie. Or maybe not.

I contacted Jones and Meredith, who were standing by in the helicopter. "Jones, are you there? Come in."

"Roger, I'm here. What's going on, Jett?" His voice was partly covered in static.

"Julie went up with Tim in the hot air balloon. Can you help them land that bloody thing?"

"I can try. Not my expertise, but I think it's fairly easy. What is her current altitude?"

I gave him the coordinates and wind speed, then signed off.

I felt helpless; I needed a driver, since I wasn't programmed to my destination. I was contemplating my next step, when I heard a motor buzzing behind me. A voice called out, "Jett, Jett, I'm here!" Pete jumped off his scooter. I automatically opened the door for him, and he slid into the driver's seat.

Breathing heavily, he said, "I got a call from Jones. He told me about Julie. I just got here after I notified the police of what was happening. They are now on alert."

"Glad you could join me, lad. Buckle up and let's play follow the leader."

Pete asked, "Where are we going?"

"We need to go to the landfill where the computers are being dumped."

"I thought Jones and Meredith were handling that."

"They're a bit busy with Julie. That's our job now."

I went into Neil's system files to get a read on the location of the dump today. The coordinates pinpointed a landfill just west of town.

Within minutes, the videophone started to ring. A look of confusion came over Pete's face. I instructed him to touch the button on the steering wheel to activate the incoming image on the computer screen. It showed Julie in the balloon, standing next to Jonathan with a nervous look on her face. How could that be? The image switched to Jones, who was filming Julie from his helicopter.

"Wanted to give you an update," Jones said. "We can't get too close because the blades might slash the balloon, but we are going to try to follow them and give them some rope to tie to the severed valve line."

"How long will that take?" I asked.

"Could be awhile with the wind shifting and blowing."

"Good luck, mates. Let me know your progress." I signed off.

The van we were following turned down a steep incline onto a road that ran along the river below. It was the same river that Julie, Gisele and Steve had rafted down. It would lead us to the landfill where Julie found the sales receipt.

Pete started to turn white.

"Pete, are you ok? You don't look good."

"Jett, I think I'm going to get sick. I'm not good in cars. I tend to get motion sickness."

"You'll need to get a hold of yourself. Do it for Julie," I said impatiently.

"Um, I guess," he replied, his voice shallow and coarse. I could feel his hands tense up on the steering wheel.

"We have to concentrate now," I said. "Stay far enough away so they can't see us, but close enough to move in when the timing is right."

Just ahead the van's brake lights illuminated and a cloud of dust spewed out from behind the tires. The driver and his helper got out, radioed to their boss that they were at the 'fill, and opened the back door exposing the load of used computers and other electronic parts. They proceeded to empty the contents onto a small flatbed vehicle.

Pete had one hand on the wheel and one on his stomach. "Jett, what do we need to do now that we are here?" he asked queasily.

"Glad you asked that, Pete, my boy. Couldn't be simpler. I'll need you to jump on the flatbed truck once they cover it. And you'll need to take your digital camera with you," I answered.

"Gotcha, I can do that," he replied with a nervous edge to his voice.

"But there's one catch, hero," I added.

"Which is?"

"You can't get caught."

"Aah, easy for you to say." Pete grunted. "Do you

have any suggestions for not getting caught?"

"Of course, Pete, hasn't Julie told you about me? I have answers. I will create a sound, which will be a diversion. As soon as they start getting curious about it, you'll need to jump on the flatbed and cover yourself with the tarp. Got it?"

The men were down to unloading the last computer and had started to shut the rear door of the van when I took charge. The noise I chose was distinct and strange at the same time. I became a moose, and not just any moose, but one who was looking for a mate. The noise was loud and disturbing. The two men stopped in their tracks and started looking around. They had a brief exchange of words and one walked slowly to the other side of the van. The second one started walking towards the landfill entrance.

Pete scrambled out and ran down behind a growth of trees. He had managed to get right near the flatbed truck when the driver, who was on the other side, reached into his pocket for his handgun. The man fired a shot into the air.

Pete froze. I realized I needed to switch the noise, or Pete might get himself into trouble. Julie would never let me live that one down.

I searched in my database of noises and found the perfect one to get this operation safely underway. A herd of cows should work. The sound penetrated the valley with loud moos and hooves stampeding the dirt. The drivers ran for cover in a small shack located just inside the gates of the landfill. Pete saw his opportunity and ran for the flatbed. He pulled the tarp over himself and secured it. I began softening the sound of the cows.

Then silence.

The men stumbled out of the shack, wiping the sweat from their brows. They hopped into the flatbed and drove it through the gates, not even taking the time to make sure that everything was secure. They drove a short way and stopped to check the location of the drop-off. Pete took this chance to crawl out from under the tarp. He quietly slid behind the back tire and waited for them to continue. When the truck began to move, he hid behind a mound of waste. The men drove the flatbed to an open area that looked as if it had just been cleared for this delivery. As soon as they started throwing the electronic parts into the shallow hole, Pete started clicking away, hiding behind the mound. Once everything had been emptied, the men turned around and drove back to the entrance. They parked the flatbed and headed for their van.

I watched with satisfaction as the lights of a police car flashed in their faces. "Police! Come out with your hands up," a voice bellowed from the loudspeaker on one of the cars.

Both men froze in their tracks and slowly put their hands up. The officers bounded out of their cars and surrounded them in seconds.

Pete staggered over to me and groped in his pocket to answer his cell phone. He tilted the phone to read a text message.

"Jett, I just got an urgent message from Gisele,"

he said breathlessly, "She's in some kind of danger at the space museum. Can you take me to her?"

"Hop in, boy, I can find her for you."

Even though we were on our way to meet Gisele, my main concern was Julie. My weather tracking system detected a lightning storm that was on the way to the exact area her balloon was headed. I needed to alert Jones about this. Balloons and dangerous weather don't go together.

Express Ride

My mind was spinning. How were we going to land? How did I get up here with, of all people, Jonathan? If only I had run to Jett instead, but I didn't want Jonathan to see Jett as a truck. I didn't want him to know we could disguise him. That was a dumb move.

The rope that Jones had been trying to get to us was swinging just beyond our reach. I looked around the tight quarters of the basket as Tim craned over the edge, frantically trying to reach the rope, our ticket to safety. Two propane tanks took up the middle of the basket, and then there was Jonathan, slumped in the corner with his arms wrapped around his knees. He was useless. If only he hadn't been obsessed with getting me in trouble, we wouldn't be in this situation. Which reminded me, where was Jett?

"Hey, Tim, do you think Jett is still at the CHIPDOME?"

He glared at me as a drop of sweat rolled down his thin nose. "Jules, I'm a bit busy right now to worry about Jett."

I turned away, embarrassed. I wished I had on my watch or some device to get in touch with him.

Wait a minute!

I stepped closer to Jonathan and said, "Do you still have my camera?"

His face was puffy and his cheeks were tear-stained. He didn't look up, but simply nodded and reached into his pocket. He held the camera far from him, as if he would catch a disease by touching it. I snatched it from him.

I gingerly walked to the other side of the basket. The "whooshing" sound of the propane filling the balloon was all I could hear. I activated the text messaging on the camera. Unfortunately, there was no audio installed on this model. I keyed in, "S.O.S. Julie"

The display screen came to life and Jett responded, "Plan A accomplished. Be aware, a storm brews on the horizon. No worries, you're in goods hands with Tim and Jones."

Suddenly, I heard a crack of thunder in the distance.

Tim's voice wavered. "Julie, did you hear that?"

I nodded slowly. Fear crept into my body. I looked around the basket and up to the balloon. In the distance, I could see huge clouds eerily waiting for us.

"Julie, listen to me." Tim grabbed my arm and shouted. "We need to act fast. If lightning should strike, it might hit the balloon, and I don't need to tell you what that means."

I reached for a stray piece of hair behind my ear and started to pull. I knew what he didn't want to say. The propane tanks could explode in mid-air if we took a lightning strike. Then, the whooshing noise stopped. I looked questioningly at Tim.

"Don't worry, the burner ran out of propane fuel. That's a good thing. It means we aren't going up any higher."

I added, "Yeah, now the wind can decide our fate."

He rolled his eyes. After a few moments the helicopter basket came close enough, and Tim got ahold of the extra rope. I helped him pull it into the basket. Jonathan glanced up, his face stone white.

"Julie, since you are lighter than I am, I'm going to need your help in attaching this rope to the valve release," Tim said. I glanced up at the broken rope, a good fifteen feet up from the basket. "Hurry up. Mother Nature is getting restless," he prodded. "And whatever you do, don't look down!"

Tim hoisted me up on top of the propane tank to angle me closer to the outside balloon rope I would use to climb up. With the storm in the distance, the wind was just starting to pick up speed. My hands were clammy and slipped at first. My arms strained as I heaved my body slowly up the rope. Finally, I reached the spot where the interior rope had snapped off. I managed to secure the valve rope with my left hand and continue to hold on tight with my right hand.

"Okay, I got it!" I yelled as I strained with every ounce of energy I had left. "What now?"

"Tie the new rope around it as tightly as you can," Tim instructed. "Once you are done, slide down the outside rope, not the one you just tied."

I did as he said, then started to slide down the outside rope. Suddenly, a burst of wind whipped through the balloon and dislodged my legs, which had been wrapped around the rope. I screamed, kicking and dangling.

Within seconds, I felt two large hands grab one of my legs. At first I thought it was Tim, but as I twisted my head around I saw in disbelief that it was Jonathan. He reached my other leg and helped pull me down the rest of the way.

I sat quietly on the floor of the basket, exhausted and stunned. Jonathan whispered, "Sorry I got you into this."

I shook my head. "Thanks for helping me."

We both looked up to see Tim pulling on the rope I had attached. The air was forced out the top of the balloon, and it began to deflate. I was expecting a sudden descent, but it was more gradual and smooth. Unfortunately, it wasn't as fast as we would have liked. The wind began to carry us further out. We could see Jones and Meredith in the helicopter, waving directions on where to land.

The thunderclouds were looming closer. I got to my feet and peered over the rim of the basket to see only forest and rock formations below us.

Crack! The thunder sounded right above the balloon. We were getting much closer to the tops of the trees. Tim looked frantic.

I reached into my pocket for the camera and saw that Jett had sent another message. It said, "Pull up on the cord and let the wind take you further out.

A landing spot is a hundred feet ahead." I motioned to Tim to ease up on the cord, and the wind managed to do its job. Sure enough, we passed over a hill, and a small clearing came into view. The sight of the grassy field raised my spirits.

Before landing, all of us wrapped our hands around the balloon ropes. I said a silent prayer for our safety. The basket bounced hard at first and my stomach flopped with it. After another bounce, the basket landed successfully upright. The deflated balloon slumped to the ground beside us. I heard the thumping noise of the helicopter, and soon saw Jones and Meredith running toward us in the distance. I smiled wearily and hugged Tim. Jonathan stood there with a look of sadness and defeat on his face.

The moment they reached us, I asked, "Where's Jett?"

Jones looked nervously at Meredith and said, "We're not sure, Julie."

The Ring Leader

"What do you mean, you don't know where Jett is?" I demanded. "I just got a text message from him right before we were about to land."

Meredith came over to me and said calmly, "I think you've had enough excitement for today. We can handle this one."

"You don't understand, something's wrong." I checked the camera again for a message. "He knew we were landing. He should have contacted us by now."

"I got a call from Pete a half hour ago, and he mentioned that they got a message from Gisele," Jones revealed. "She wanted Pete to meet her at a space museum."

"Does anyone know where that is?" Meredith asked.

"Yes, I have the map from Neil's office." I reached into my pocket to pull out the wrinkled map.

Jones cleared his throat and said with determination, "Excellent, let's take the helicopter. Jonathan we'll need you to stay by the balloon."

Everyone sprinted to the helicopter. Just as Jones closed the door, a loud clap of thunder erupted, and the rain started coming down in buckets. The storm was upon us. Jones switched the power on, and we heard the swift rush of the blades as they started rotating. He reached under his seat and put on his earphones and handed a set for each of us to put on.

In a matter of minutes, we were flying directly above an oval-shaped building. It stood proudly on a hill overlooking a dried-up creek bed to one side and an evergreen forest on the other.

The building had huge ceiling-to-floor windows all the way around; even the doors were glass. The second floor was also glassed in and housed a large telescope that peered out of the middle and tilted up to the sky.

"Wow, cool place," Tim said.

I asked Jones for some bino glasses, the latest form of optical magnification. I scanned the area and saw some tire tracks. I zoomed in closer and was pretty sure I recognized them: Jett tracks.

Jett Log 15.00 hours

The museum location blinked on the screen as I drove us closer to it. Pete had gotten over his motion sickness and was humming along to some pop music he requested me to play.

I hadn't heard from Julie since the message I sent her through the camera. I wished she was with me. I couldn't believe I even liked a human besides PJ.

"Slow down," Pete said, interrupting my thoughts. After a quick turn onto a dirt driveway lined with willow trees, a large glassed-in building came into view. "I'm going to pull over here," Pete said. He pointed to a clear patch under a grove of trees.

"Let's make sure Gisele is here," I said, activating the heat-seeking sensor in my computer. There were people in the building all right. I could make out the outline of three figures in the basement. I showed them to Pete. "Looks like she isn't alone."

"I'm going to check it out. I should be right back," he said.

"Pete, please be..." He had already slammed the door. I watched as he ambled up the hill to the museum.

Bloody kids, he was just like Julie, bolting off without heeding my advice. I would have to ask PJ to devise a seat belt that I could control to tie them down. Ah, but more importantly, I needed to check on Julie. My satellite scan showed that they were approaching the landing site, but they seemed too close to the tree line. I was readying a message to alert them to the clearing, when my sensors picked up movement in the distance.

*　*　*　*　*　*　*　*

I jumped down from the helicopter and covered my ears from the noise. The plan was that I would go into the museum first. If I was in danger, I would send a signal, or if I took too long, they'd come investigate.

We needed to land the helicopter far away in order to go undetected. I had to run at least a mile to get near the perimeter. By the time I came to the trees that surrounded the building, I was out of breath and soaking wet.

Suddenly the wristwatch that Jones gave me started to vibrate. A text message read: 'Pete in danger. Jett in woods. East side of museum.'

I veered off behind the building and located Jett parked a hundred yards away behind a large pine tree. I sighed as I jumped inside. "Jett, it's so good to see you!"

"Julie, we have no time for chit chat. Your friend Pete is in trouble. You must go get him while I guide the police to this spot."

"Why did you let him go in there by himself?"

"Unfortunately, he's like you. He acts before listening. He ran off before I could reason with him."

I nodded slowly. "I'm ready to go in. What do you suggest I do first?"

"Pete is in the basement. He is not alone. I'm not sure if he is tied up or if they are surrounding him. Show them the map that you have and throw it at them. When they try to get it, grab Pete and run. By that time, the police should be here."

"How important is the map?"

"It shows where the previous owners of the building buried the recipe for zicanium."

"Wow! So that's what Meredith must have been talking about, except she didn't even know the name." I grabbed a piece of hair from behind my ear and started twirling it tightly.

"She was close; it is the product of melting down mercury, found in computers, titanium, and copper. The key is that it needs to mix with the soil. Thus, the reason why they don't recycle the electronic parts to begin with. In essence, they are farming a new lethal powder."

"So, how does it work?" I stammered.

"If they mix too much soil, it turns into dust. If not

enough, it dissolves in water. But if mixed correctly, it is powerful enough to send a rocket ship to the moon, or, in the wrong hands, as Meredith said, it could cause an explosion that could take out a large city, " Jett said.

"Okay, I've got it — pressure's on! Let me go get Pete." My mind whirred as I opened the door. I tiptoed over to the rear entrance, which was luckily unlocked, and slipped inside. Murals of the solar system were mounted on the walls and glowing yellow arrows had been set in the floor to guide people from room to room. I tiptoed across the bright white tile floor, and then gasped. A headless space suit was floating up in the corner. Must be recovering from a bad moon landing, I thought with a grin.

Suddenly, I heard muffled voices below me. I scanned the room and saw a blue door marked "Employees Only" on the far wall.

My rain-soaked shoes squeaked as I walked through the museum. I pulled them off, before slowly opening the door and then crept down the stairs. When I reached the bottom, my eyes had to adjust to the dimly lit room. As I squinted, I saw in the far corner, Gisele, her father, and Neil surrounding Pete, who was sitting on the floor with his head hung low.

I couldn't help but notice Gisele's hair was a mess. This was out of character for a girl who had to match every outfit down to her toenails. The pants she was wearing had to be a few years old, and her sneakers even had mud on them. I froze in place and listened to their conversation.

"What brings you here, Gisele?" her father asked. "I thought you didn't know how to get here."

"Steve showed me the route. Hey, what's he doing here?" Her eyes darted from her father to Pete.

"We need him to get us back the map." Neil snarled, wiping his brow and dusting off his leather pants.

"You kidnapped one of my friends? First, you lied about Mr. Avalon even existing to cover your operation, and now this?" She stamped her foot on the dirty floor, and pressed her hands to her hips.

"Gisele, honey, how can you be so naive?" asked her father. "I don't need anyone meddling in my business. No one will say I'm damaging the environment once they find out how lucrative this mixture can be."

Neil added coyly, "Do you want your daddy to go out of business and not be able to buy you pretty clothes?"

She started to wipe her face, and I realized she was crying. She softly said, "I hate that you do this. And I hate that you forced me to spy on Julie from the beginning."

Mr. Nickels replied impatiently, "Then help me understand. What's the problem? You said she was a geek."

"The fact is, I really do like her."

I felt stunned by her confession, but before I could think, Neil, shouted, "What are we going to do with the boy?"

Mr. Nickels wheeled around, pumped his hands in the air, and hooted, "To the roof, Neil! To the roof!"

I froze. Should I act now or when they take him to

the roof? I wish I could have spoken with Jett one more time. I had better do something before it's too late.

I dove out from behind the staircase. "Stop right there." I shouted.

Neil's face turned white. Mr. Nickels grabbed Gisele by the wrist and Pete jolted upright and grinned.

I dangled the map in front of them. "Is this what you were looking for?" Before I could throw down the map and run to Pete, Neil reached into his pocket and pulled out a gun. Gisele and I gasped at the same time.

"I've been meaning to do this from the very beginning." Neil said, looking straight at Mr. Nickels. "You think you dreamed up this entire idea, when in reality, it was all me. Now it's time to pay." The pistol slipped slightly in his hand and he used his other hand to steady it.

"Neil, don't be silly; you couldn't have done this without my financial support," Mr. Nickels said calmly. As they started to banter back and forth, I eyed Pete and motioned my head slightly to the exit.

Neil whirled around and waved the gun at me, "No motions there, young lady. Drop the map on the floor in front of you, and then I want everyone on the roof. Move!"

We started up the steps single file, reaching the ground floor, then turned to follow a narrow stairway all the way to the roof. Neil's eyes were wild and his whole body trembled as he prodded us to the top.

The roof held an enormous telescope. It was aimed toward the sky, greeting it with a watchful eye. The view was astonishing. I could see the hills and fields for miles around.

Neil had us stop midway. Beads of sweat were running down the side of his face and he had to wipe his face with his sleeve. "I want all the kids together. Mr. Nickels, you stay where you are." He shoved us together, and we grabbed on to each other to make sure none of us went over the edge.

The noise of the helicopter throbbed in our ears, and we bowed down as it dipped close to the roof. It was Jones.

The helicopter diverted everyone's attention and it gave me a moment to peer over the edge to see where Jett was. He had activated the mattress-like cushion on the flatbed of his truck frame. If I wanted to escape, that was where I needed to land.

Neil reeled at the sight of the helicopter and shouted, "Who is trying to get me?"

Suddenly a voice that sounded familiar bellowed behind us, "Neil, put down the gun, you've done enough harm already." Gil was standing by the entrance to the telescope on the far end of the roof. "I've uncovered the recipe without the map. I beat you to it."

Neil's face turned white and then he lunged at me and grabbed me by the arm. "Drop your gun or she dies."

The pistol was pointed at my head. My heart started racing and my vision started to blur. All I could hear was the helicopter blades in the distance.

Gisele made a high-pitched scream and all eyes turned to her. This confused Neil and he didn't anticipate Mr. Nickels coming up from behind.

The impact of Mr. Nickels on his back forced the gun from Neil's hand and over the edge of the roof. Everything happened so quickly, the next thing I knew was that I was plummeting through the air and landing in a large cushion. I opened my eyes and realized Pete and Gisele had grabbed me to make the leap off the roof.

A police siren sounded, and I looked up to see them closing in and swarming the building. Jones landed the helicopter on the front lawn.

Suddenly, a bolt of lightning came out of the sky and hit the telescope with a crack. We looked up to the roof to see Mr. Nickels and Gil run for the stairs, but Neil was too slow to respond and the electric jolt from the telescope took him down.

Gisele and I gasped and by then, the police had taken over the building.

I didn't realize that I had been shaking until Pete handed me a blanket and said, "Are you okay?"

"Yeah, but I can't say the same for our villains."

I turned my attention to Gisele, who looked relieved in an odd sort of way. She winked at me and rested her head on Jett's hood with outstretched arms.

"Jett saved us," she said happily. "He's the best."

Headliner

Pete shifted slightly in the torn overstuffed chair that was positioned near his desk. His bedroom walls were covered with layers of posters and newspaper headlines. The harsh tapping sounds of the keyboard made me think of a newsroom.

I sat on the carpeted floor and sipped an iced tea as his tuxedo cat, Reynolds, rubbed against my elbow for attention.

I grinned at Gisele, who sat cross-legged on Pete's bed waving her hands wildly in the air — her favorite way to dry her polished fingers.

"Pete, don't leave us in suspense. What's the name of the lead story you're writing for the school paper?" I asked.

"*A Landfill Mystery: Solved* — What do you think?"

I sighed. "That's kind of boring. Gisele and I will think of something more exciting."

"Good idea, but we need something to spur ideas," Gisele said.

"Pete, why don't you interview us?" I asked.

Pete faced us, pointed his pen at me, "Good idea." He cleared his voice and began, "When did you realize that the illegal dumping of electronic products was tied to Neil at the CHIPDOME?"

"First, Jett did a search on the company Neil said they used for the recycling. Nothing came up, which was suspicious."

"How did you know for sure?" he prodded.

"The day Gisele, Steve, and I went rafting, I stumbled upon a phony receipt in another landfill near the river. It had Neil's signature on it."

"That's when you went snooping in Neil's office. Which was so cool," Gisele added, playing with her hair.

"And you discovered the map to the museum, correct?"

"Yes."

"Why did Neil become partners with Mr. Nickels to begin with?"

"Mr. Nickels gave Neil the money to build the space museum, a common interest they had. Neil became obsessed with it and he convinced himself it was his idea. He's a creep through and through!"

Pete continued, "This Jett car that you drive, how did it help you to find the culprits?"

"Jett knew all along that we needed to focus on finding the mastermind. Mr. Nickels thought he could take advantage of dumping electronics and mine it for this magic powder, and, in the end, to make loads of money. Jett provided the necessary information to frame all of the players. Neil and Gil were just in it for the fringe benefits."

"Pretty impressive, for a car," Pete replied. "Did the

electronics that were dumped, harm the water supply?"

"The jury is still out on that. I think we caught the dumping in time, however, they are doing extensive testing just to make sure."

I looked at Gisele and remembered what I had been itching to ask her, "Gis, why did you swipe my disk in the bathroom at school?"

Her eyes twinkled and she grinned for an instant. "My father kept talking about your car, and I knew it was more than curiosity. When you told me about the disk, I realized that was my chance to help out — to stop him from doing any more harm."

Pete glanced up from his computer. "Speaking of which, what type of punishment will your father get?"

"He'll be in jail for a year and have to do community service for another year. Since he had no prior criminal record, he was given a light sentence."

Pete nodded sympathetically, then asked, "Julie, what are your plans?"

"The Recycle Council started an electronic recycling program for the town. I'm also making Gisele an honorary member." I winked at her.

"By the way, whatever happened with Jonathan?" Pete asked casually.

"He sent me this." I reached into my pocket and pulled out a silver locket. Gisele grabbed it and opened it up. She pushed the button on the side, and a ten-second video of Jett played. "Oh, that is sweet of him," she cooed.

"He also included a handwritten note that read,

'sorry' in capital letters and signed his name," I said.

"Sounds to me like he's starting to like you." Pete sighed.

I rolled my eyes. "It's not me he likes, it's Jett."

"What? I don't believe you. We'll need to spy on his computer at school. He probably saved your picture as a screensaver!" Gisele screeched.

"Very funny." I pulled on a piece of hair behind my ear.

Pete leaned over to me and squeezed my hand. "You're cute when you get embarrassed."

I pulled my hand away and quickly said, "How about *Uncovering Mercury Mountain?*" I offered.

"For what?" Pete asked.

"The title for your article. Remember?"

"Right. I like it!" He straightened up in his chair and turned to Gisele. "How about you?"

"That's perfect!" Gisele said, clapping her manicured hands.

"There's something we're forgetting to do," I said, as I pointed out the window. "We need to ask Jett."

Pete typed a message on his computer. Seconds later, a screen popped up. We stared at it. It read, "Sounds completely, bloody terrible. Jett."

"I guess he doesn't like it," Gisele said with a sigh.

"Oh no, that's just Jett-speak. He totally digs it!" I said as I ran to the window to see him parked in the driveway.

Before I stepped away, I heard the sound of a high-powered engine and turned my attention to see Steve pull into the driveway in his cool convertible. He looked up and waved at me. My heart skipped a beat and I smiled a second before Gisele came running up next to me. "What is my brother doing here? I didn't call him or anything."

"Gis, he called me," I replied.

Jett Log: 12.00 hrs.

Well, mates, there you have it. My first eco-adventure with Julie and my new friends and family. At first, I have to say, I was incredibly unhappy being locked up in that cluttered garage, but as luck would have it, that all changed. I never imagined our first case would take place in Julie's hometown. Because I was built for speed, I thought we would be far, far away from home, catching environmental thieves. It just goes to show that people who abuse and poison our planet for their own benefit could be right next-door.

The other thing I was amazed at was the dedication of everyone at E.V.E.N., including Julie's family and friends. I was leery of people from the beginning, but now I think I actually like them. I know, scary, isn't it?

I hope you enjoyed our tale, and if you get anything out of it, remember, beware of tall poppies and make sure you recycle!

Cheers, Jett

Ways You Can Help

RECYCLING

Recycle City .... **www.epa.gov/recyclecity**
Computer Take Back Campaign ....**www.computertakeback.com**
Ollie Recycles .... **www.olliesworld.com/recycle**
Rechargeable Battery Recycling Corporation .... **www.rbrc.org**

GENERAL ENVIRONMENTAL SITES

Earth Day .... **www.earthday.com**
Going Places, Making Choices:
Transportation and the Environment **www.4hgpmc.com**
Kids Saving the Planet .... **www.kidssavingtheplanet.org**
EPA Explorers' Club .... **www.epa.gov/kids/index.htm**
EPA Student Center.................................... **www.epa.gov/students**
Planet Protectors Club .... **www.epa.gov/epaoswer/osw/kids**
Adventure Ecology .... **www.adventureecology.com**

GROUNDWATER POLLUTION

Water Environment Federation..................................... **www.wef.org**

MERCURY AWARENESS

Mercury Education for Kids ....
            www.epa.gov/superfund/kids/sup_fact/mercury1.htm

ASSOCIATIONS

National Resources Defense Council .... **www.nrdc.org**
National Recycling Coalition .... **www.nrc-recycle.org**
The Nature Conservancy .... **www.nature.org**

ENVIRONMENTAL BLOG

Chat the Planet....................................... **www.chattheplanet.com**

Key Terms

Altitude: the height measured above sea level.

Biodegradable: materials that can be broken down by bacteria from the environment.

Cadmium: a grayish chemical element that looks like tin and is used in producing batteries and other electronic components.

Carbon Monoxide: a colorless, odorless, poisonous gas that is the largest pollutant emitted by cars.

Decompose: to decay or break down to parts that can be reused by other plants or animals.

Electronic Recycling: a form of recycling specifically designed to reuse parts from electronics such as computers, TVs, cell phones, and other electronic products.

Emissions Standards: air quality regulations that limit the amount of pollutants that vehicles are allowed to produce.

Fossil Fuels: oil that comes from the decay of former plants and animals over millions of years.

Fuel Cell: a chemical process that converts fuel into electrical energy without combustion.

Groundwater: water lying below the earth's surface that can be found in either springs or pores of rock.

Greenhouse Gases: gases released from cars, factories, and companies into the atmosphere that combine with the heat of the earth and contribute to global warming.

Hybrid: something made by combining two different elements.

Hydrocarbons: the second largest group of pollutants produced by cars (made up of hydrocarbon + carbon atoms).

Hydrogen: a colorless, odorless, gaseous element that combines with oxygen to form water.

Industrial Waste: waste produced by factories and manufacturing companies – often poisonous.

Landfill: an area of land designed to safely store decomposing trash.

Leachate: a product resulting from rotting garbage mixed with rainwater.

Lead: a heavy metallic element.

Mercury: a heavy metal (and neuro toxin) that can accumulate in the environment and is highly toxic if breathed or swallowed.

Monitoring Wells: a system of wells around a landfill that detects any contamination to the groundwater supply.

Municipal Waste: waste gathered by a town or city government.

Nitrogen Oxide: a compound of nitrogen and oxygen – contributes to smog.

Toxin: a poisonous substance.

Zero-emission: produces no pollutants into the air.

To purchase additional copies of this book
and for more information on the environment visit:
www.indiaevansbooks.com